THE RENEGADES

Book Two: Aftermath

JACK HUNT

DIRECT RESPONSE PUBLISHING

Published by Direct Response Publishing

ISBN-13: 978-1523628193
ISBN-10: 1523628197

Also By Jack Hunt

The Renegades
The Renegades 2: Aftermath

Dedication

For Dax, Baja, Specs, Jess, Izzy, Ralphie, Ben and Elijah

Prologue

"Johnny, are you sure this camera's working?"

I cleared my throat. Okay, so it's finally happened! The shit has really hit the fan. I'm talking about an out of control, fasten your seat belt and don't forget to bring a spare pair of underpants, kind of deal.

That's right — America is now knee-deep in a zombie apocalypse.

But before we get to the juicy part about how some idiot hit the wrong button, I should probably bring you up to speed on what triumphant acts occurred prior to penning this beauty.

Now, my friend Johnny wanted me to leave this

part out — but like I told him. If I'm gonna die, you can bet your ass I want the world to know about our heroic deeds. I mean, who knows? Maybe it will go viral, if they ever get the power back up.

By the way, I'm Nick Halliway, or as my friends like to call me, Baja, after I took my parents' 1979 Country Squire station wagon for an off-road joyride at the age of twelve.

What an epic moment that was.

In fact, do you know I can still hear the sirens of the boys in blue ringing in my ears six years later?

Ah...good times!

Anyway, back to this hellish nightmare that we find ourselves in.

After all hell broke loose in our small town of Castle Rock, Nevada, we lost Matt our closest friend and pretty much every family member. We encountered a bunch of pyschobillies being led by an asshole who called himself the Colonel. We rescued two local girls who were being held captive, and I hung from a wire over a sinkhole caused by igniting one-hundred-year-old dynamite. Which by the way blew up half the town.

"Baja! You didn't hang from the wire, I did," Johnny hollered from his bed in a motel room.

"You say tomato, I say tomahto. Why are we splitting hairs here?"

"Listen, I told you that you could do the first part of this story on one condition — that you tell the truth."

"This is the truth. Alright, hypothetically it wasn't me hanging there, but our lives were hanging in the balance, so… it kind of was me."

"It wasn't."

"It was."

Whatever. So we are currently on our way to Salt Lake City in the grand hope of finding a safe zone with bunch of folks who don't want to take a chunk out of our ass. Personally, I'm just hoping the safe zone isn't some biker bar full of greasy ass motherfuckers who just escaped from prison. As I, for one, am not bunking with anyone by the name of Bubba.

So the world's gone to hell and somehow we've managed to survive.

Now, I'm sure you're thinking why us? To be honest, I'm not sure.

But, I'll leave the rest of the story for Johnny to tell.

Signing out for now. This is Nick "Baja" Halliway, the one who will eventually save the world. You have my word on that!

"Baja!"

"Okay, I gotta go."

THE HERD

A lot of shit can happen over the course of five hundred and twenty-four miles. That was the distance between Castle Rock and Salt Lake City. We had driven east, taken the I-80 without knowing what to expect. What should have been eight hours with minimal traffic took days. It was far worse than we had imagined. For as far as the eye could see, flames smoldered furiously from vehicles, bodies lay in various stages of decomposition, while the undead moved like an army.

The first five nights we holed up in a rundown motel called the Wagon Safari just on the outskirts of Lovelock, Nevada. I wanted to keep moving but Dax insisted we stay. I still had wounds that needed to heal, he said. I was sure that the damage was bad because my pant legs were soaked in blood. Thankfully the first bullet hadn't hit a major artery or bone. It hadn't even got lodged in my thigh. It was a clean shot. The second had only grazed my calf. Regardless, the scarring would be brutal. After being sewn up, I spent the next five days resting. We took turns keeping watch while others slept. It was a painful time but I was lucky to have made it out with all my limbs intact.

Once we got back on the road, I was just glad to get the hell out of there. There had been a few close calls, and everyone was starting to get a little anxious. Our fears weren't just of encountering more Z's but the living insane. The crazies. Those who knew nothing more than killing.

We traveled for another day. It was slow and all of us were worn out.

I jolted awake to the warmth of the cab.

"Johnny, you okay?"

I blinked hard.

"Yeah."

I wondered if the Colonel had survived. Several nights I had dreamt of him crawling out of that hole. Each time I would see him reach the top. He would fix his milky white gaze on me. Blood gushed from his mouth as he'd claw his way towards me. I never saw what happened next as I would wake up sweating profusely.

None of us had spoken about what went down in Castle Rock. In many ways we were still in shock trying to come to terms with the fact that our lives would never be the same again.

I gazed out the window. It was close to midnight. We had been on the road for hours, and yet barely made any progress in reaching the city. The truck wound its way around vehicles that were clogging up the highway. You couldn't exactly drive in a line. There were too many abandoned. As we came over a rise in the road we saw what looked like a twenty vehicle pileup. Dax made a decision to rest there for the night, siphon vehicles of gas, and look for food. We had done it several times. That night it was a big mistake.

* * *

Twenty minutes later, I inhaled hard trying to catch my breath. A flurry of anxious thoughts assaulted me as I lay beneath a burnt out 4 x 4 truck, staring at Jess and Izzy who had squeezed under a camper trailer. The sounds of moaning filled the air. It had been peaceful for a while. Baja and Specs were going from vehicle to vehicle removing as much as gas as they could with some plastic tubing. Jess and Izzy searched vehicles for food while I kept a lookout. Millie and Caitlin were asleep inside the truck. Dax had told me to stay off the leg for at least another week, but that had gone over about as well as most of his commands.

There was an eerie feel to being out in the middle of a highway at night. Add to that seeing vehicles abandoned and the knowledge that people didn't just vanish. It had all of us on high alert. Suitcases were littered all over the place. Any food that I had found in previous days had become rotten. We now searched for canned goods or anything with high sodium content. Anything that might last longer than its expiration date. Both sides of the road were hedged in by a thick pine forest, behind that were snow-peaked mountains. Most of the time we had to drive on the hard shoulder because of how badly the roads were clogged up. Even then it was like navigating our way through a minefield. Sometimes we had to get out and push cars out of the way. Other times we just plowed through them. You never quite knew what you were going to encounter next. I'd like to say we were adapting to our new way of living but we weren't.

Once again we were facing the dead. Initially I thought it was just one; a straggler that had emerged from the forest. It soon turned into two, three, and then an entire herd broke out of the tree line. There was no time to shout. Dax was further down the road keeping an eye on that end. The two girls were somewhere in the middle and Baja and Specs were closest to me.

I slid off the roof and hightailed it over to Baja. He

was making some joke about the way Specs was sucking at the tube. After alerting them, Specs shot over to Jess. Izzy whistled to Dax and all of us hit the floor. We scrambled under the closest vehicles and waited. Now you would think that would keep us safe, but it doesn't. It wasn't the first time we had to do it. The last time was about an hour outside of Castle Rock. I was still bleeding back then, and I swear they could smell fresh blood because as I lay quietly beneath a truck, a meaty hand tried to grab me. Luckily Dax was there and he gave the Z a third eye. All of us knew the plan. If you ever got into a bind, you were to cover yourself in zombie guts. It didn't always work but it increased the odds of surviving. Right now there was no time to do that.

As we waited under the vehicles for the herd to pass by, what we hadn't anticipated was Caitlin and Millie waking up. They were completely oblivious to what was taking place. It was Caitlin's voice I heard first, then her scream.

"Guys? Anyone?"

There was no way of knowing if she had been bit or not. I couldn't get out even if I wanted to, as both sides of the truck I was under were blocked by Z's. Helplessly, I listened to her screaming. Then I heard bullets. All I could see in the darkness were legs. It was like a human centipede. Most shuffled, others moved fast making their way in the direction of her voice.

Then it went dead silent. My eyes remained on Jess and Izzy. Both of them looked scared. We waited until there were no more Z's passing before inching out. Further down, Dax was already out. He retracted his knife from the skull of a Z. Its body flopped to the ground. He stared down, paying no attention to us coming up from the rear.

As I drew closer I noticed what he was staring at. It was Millie. My eyes darted to the truck. Inside Caitlin was sobbing her eyes out. I didn't even need to motion to Jess. She and Izzy were already opening the door and trying to console her. She was beside herself. So choked up she couldn't even get a word out. When the words came, they were pushed through tears and gasps for air.

"Slow down, take a deep breath," Izzy said.

In the distance we could see a few of the remaining herd disappearing into the tree line. They had crossed from one side to the next. That was it. But in the process they had taken another life. We had barely had the chance to get to know Millie.

Now, we wouldn't.

Dax didn't wait for her to turn. He ran his knife into Millie's forehead. Thankfully Caitlin didn't see it. Baja grabbed a blanket from a vehicle and covered her corpse. It had been a while since we had lost anyone. It once again was a wakeup call to all of us to be vigilant. It could have been any of us.

We didn't stay there any longer. Not that we couldn't have locked ourselves in the truck. But the majority wanted to move on. Psychologically we didn't know how death affected any of us. Each of us was dealing with the loss of our families in our own way. But none of us except Dax and I had witnessed a family member being eaten alive. Caitlin was already suffering from her time in the silo. They had murdered her father, and now her sister was dead.

"Specs, gather the cans of gasoline. We are moving out."

He nodded and Baja went with him.

I knew the moment we were all inside the truck, Dax would begin. He'd been holding it back since Castle Rock but I could tell he was just waiting for the right time.

"We need some ground rules," he said.

"Oh great," I heard Baja mutter.

"We stick together in twos. None of us ventures out without informing whoever is staying behind as to your whereabouts."

It was a little too late.

We later learned from Jess that Caitlin and Millie had stepped out either side of the vehicle. Millie was bitten before her sister could do anything. By the time she reacted she had no other option than to dive back into the truck or she would have died too.

It was quiet in the truck as we continued on our way. Specs had retrieved very little gas from the vehicles, and what he had managed to store in a container was knocked over when the herd came through. We were getting used to living on very little. Most of the time you could hear our stomachs rumble. As strange as it may sound, in the first few days after leaving Castle Rock, there would be an air of excitement, accomplishment even, when a Z was killed. Maybe because we thought we were ridding the world of the infected. It soon dissipated, as it became the norm. Soon what little discussion we had between us was about what we needed: food, supplies, and directions. We pushed through each day as we made our way to Salt Lake City.

THE HITCHER

I thought I had seen it all but clearly not.

Now my father would say there were only three rules a man should live by. Never turn down a drink, always wear a hat on your bat, and whatever the fuck you do, don't pick up a hitcher.

I knew we should have listened to him.

"Guys, you just drove past someone." Jess thumbed over her shoulder.

"I didn't see anyone, did you?" Baja asked.

I cast a glance to my left and right. "Nah," I replied with a smirk.

Now the guy was no ordinary hitcher sticking out his thumb. He was all arms and legs. Running for his life from a group of eight Z's. Imagine a beached whale. You got that? That would be kind of close to what this guy looked like. There was a whole lot of junk in his trunk. We would have left him far behind if it wasn't for Jess and Izzy. Their hearts were bigger than their brains, Baja told them later. Oh, don't worry, he has a bruised arm to remind him never to say that out loud. Nine times out of ten he was wrong, but in this instance, he was right on the money.

She tapped Dax on the arm. "Dax, stop."

Now Dax at the best of times doesn't like people telling him what to do. I haven't a clue how the hell he made his way through boot camp. The guy was hard-wired to say *no* to practically anything except a pair of legs in a skirt. He continued driving until the constant nagging from Jess and Izzy made him slam the brakes on. We all jerked forward, nearly embedding our teeth into the interior. He shifted into reverse until he was within a few feet of the guy.

Jess cracked the door.

He waved us on. "Go. Go, I'll jump in the back."

Dax waited until we heard the sound of a thud

landing in the back. I swear we caught some air and experienced for a few brief seconds what it must have been like to be in zero gravity. There was no time to adjust to our new visitor as two of the Z's were already clambering onto the back of the truck.

"Ahhh, help," the guy screamed.

Specs and I jumped out. Specs fired a round into one of their heads. I took out the other one. It had a hold of him and was scraping at the guy's clothes when I slammed the knife into the back of its head. I yanked it out and some of the blood flicked onto him. You should have heard him scream. It was unnatural. Like a five-year-old having their rattle taken from them.

"Get it off. Get it off," he yelled.

Meanwhile Specs and Jess took out three more Z's.

"Calm down."

He was pushing back at the Z with his feet and trying to wipe the blood. Even when it was gone and all that remained was a smear he still screamed. Jess was wide-eyed. Baja was roaring with laughter. I jumped up onto the truck bed and he raised his hands, cowering back as though I was about to knife him.

"It's okay." I slotted the blade back into the sheath on my thigh and held up my hands so he could see I was no threat.

"Please. Get this off."

Tears were pouring down his face.

"Get what off?"

He stared at his hand as if he had contracted some foreign disease.

"The blood? You can't turn from having their blood on you."

He nodded. "Yes. You can."

Specs frowned and twirled his finger around near his own ear as if to indicate the guy had lost his marbles. For a moment I did think of just tossing him from the truck. Who knew what trouble he could give us? I certainly didn't like the idea of some head case being close to Jess.

I took a hold of his hands and brought them

together but he wrestled them from my grip. He kept staring at them. So I did what any logical person does when someone is acting like a complete loon. I slapped him.

"Snap out of it, you idiot."

And like that the guy seemed to come to his senses.

"Johnny!" Jess said in protest.

I shrugged.

"The old slap him silly trick," Baja muttered. "Shit, I should have thought of that. It's a lot of fun too," he said before giving Specs a slap as he hopped back into the cab.

"Dude, what the hell?" Specs griped.

Baja chuckled.

Once I was satisfied the guy wasn't going to lose it — I joined the others inside.

When I jumped in the suspension barely moved. It was already squished to its max. I had visions of the back tires being stuck in mud with all that weight, thankfully that wasn't the case. Dax gunned it before the others who were dragging ass caught up.

"Be nice," Jess said to me. I rolled my eyes.

She slid back the window on the cab.

"Hey thanks, I thought I was going to become zombie chow back there."

"What's your name?"

"Ralph, but my pals call me..."

He paused for a second to catch his breath. Baja jumped on it.

"...dumbass?" Baja added.

Izzy slapped him.

"Shit, Izzy, you need to ease up."

"My pals call me Ralphie."

"I would have never guessed that," Specs muttered.

"Where you from?" Dax yelled from the front. Ralphie stuck his head into the opening, filling what little space there was with skin.

"Wells."

"You?" he asked.

"Castle Cock," Baja said, lighting a cigarette.

"Ignore him, he has mental problems," Izzy said glaring at Baja.

Ralphie's eyes darted between all of us.

"Wells, Nevada. We'll be passing through there on the way to Salt Lake City."

"Not much left. I barely managed to escape."

Suddenly, Dax slammed the brakes on and jumped out.

"Strip down," he said to Ralphie.

"What?"

"You heard me."

I ducked my head out the window.

"Okay, Dax, I know you've always been one for the lads. There's no shame in that, but eh, I think you might want to go on a first date."

"At least buy him flowers," Baja added.

Dax rolled his eyes. "I'm checking for bites, morons."

"I'm not bitten."

Dax motioned with his Glock for him to get out of

the back. Once again we had to feel our stomachs fly up into our throats as Ralphie hopped off the back of the truck. He glanced at Jess, Izzy, and Caitlin and went a deep shade of red.

"Dax, is this really necessary?" Izzy asked.

Dax ignored her. His eyes were fixed on Ralphie who was sweating and looking dark around the eyes. He had a point. We had no idea if one of those Z's had taken a chunk out of him. We were surprised that he had even managed to outrun them.

"Do you even remember seeing him by the side of the road?" Specs asked me.

"What do you mean?" I said quietly.

"If I wasn't mistaken he just appeared out of nowhere."

While we were talking Ralphie had begun stripping down to his tighty-whiteys. Baja started swirling his groin around while hollering, "Key the music. Yeah! Magic Mike is in the house. Bust a move."

"Sit the hell down," Dax yelled.

I think I actually caught Izzy smirk which only made Ralphie go a deeper shade of red.

Dax walked around him.

"Like what you see?" I shouted to Dax. Dax flipped me the bird.

"Skiddddyyy," Baja yelled, referring to the brown trace of shit on the poor guy's underpants.

"Baja, I swear you have the mind of a twelve-year-old."

"Sweet cheeks, admit it. You have a thing for me," Baja replied back.

Izzy screwed up her face and threw up her middle finger.

"All right. Sorry to make you do that. But we have to be careful," Dax said.

Ralphie pulled his clothes on like an embarrassed young virgin and Dax got back into the truck.

"Here. You might want this." Jess shoved her coat through the window. It was cold outside. Just with the windows down we were getting chilled. I had visions of arriving in Salt Lake City and Ralphie frozen to death in the back of the truck. As soon as he was back in, Dax floored it.

I looked over his shoulder and could see we were down to a quarter of a tank of gas. Definitely not enough to get us to the city.

"We need to stop for gas."

Dax glanced down. "We'll try the next town."

"There's nothing there. I saw it on my way out. It's been looted," Ralphie said. "In fact, you're better off giving Wells a wide berth too. A lot of asshats there."

Dax eyed him in his rearview mirror. I could tell he was skeptical of our new addition. We all were. It wasn't that we weren't open to have another with us. In all honesty it was a good thing. Baja had leaned back and asked me what I thought of having him tagging along. I told him it was one more person to fire a gun. He replied, "Yeah. I guess in the worst-case scenario, we could feed him to the Z's and make a run for it." He grinned. I could always trust Baja to find some odd angle.

We drove a few more miles until we came across the town that Ralphie was on about. It was called Halleck, Nevada. He wasn't kidding. The place was a total ghost town. It consisted of two buildings: a post office and a gas station. Dax slowed down to a crawl while we took in the sight of the burnt-out post office.

"Shit, and there was me thinking of sending a postcard back to Castle Rock," Specs said.

The gas station was in a far worse state. A truck had been driven right into the single gas pump they had. What remained of it lay black and burnt. The building had been leveled by the explosion. None of the charred bodies appeared to be moving.

"You think we have enough to make it to Wells?"

"How far is it from here, Ralphie?" Dax asked.

He pushed his face through the open slot like an eager pug dog.

"It's a thirty-minute drive."

Dax sniffed hard. "I guess we should have enough. There's gas stations there, yeah?"

"How are you going to get gas out of them if there is no electricity?" Ralphie asked.

"Couple of ways. Open the covers where they refill the tanks. Unless the underground containers have been destroyed, there is going to be some inside. Or you can get the side covers off the gas pumps and then slip a hose and siphon out that way," Specs said as he continued to try the portable radio for a signal.

"I just think you'd be better off going around Wells."

That was it. Dax stopped the vehicle and turned in his seat.

"What are you not telling us?"

"Just saying. It's probably best you avoid Wells."

"What is there?"

Ralphie gulped. His eyes dropped.

"You want to walk?" Dax said.

"Dax," I said.

"No," he spat back. "If we are driving into an ambush. I want to know."

"It's not an ambush. But let's just say the people have gone a little crazy there."

"How crazy?"

Ralphie slumped back down, not wanting to answer that.

"Let me handle this," I said. Dax shook his head.

I hopped out of the truck and came around to the side. I gazed out at the desert that was now covered in snow. The clouds had come down so it looked almost like a fine mist was hovering above the ground. I leaned against the truck, nodded to Jess and she pulled the sliding rear window closed.

"Listen. We've lost a lot of people: family, friends. Forgive my brother for being a little cautious but you aren't the first person we have allowed to get close only to have them screw us over. Now if there is anything we need to know before driving through that town, you need to tell us now, because..." I scratched the side of my head. "I might let it slide. But my brother, he's liable to put a bullet in your head if he thinks for one moment you are up to something."

"I'm not. I just don't want to go back there."

"But you knew we were heading that way."

"Yeah, but I thought you might be taking a different route."

"Ralphie, do you have any family?"

His eyes dropped. He shook his head.

"How did you lose them?"

He cleared his throat, looked out, and shivered slightly.

"My father was the first to turn."

He had this faraway look in his eyes as if he was recalling everything that had taken place.

"I had two sisters, one brother. All of them died. I saw him kill them all. I can still hear their screams." He paused and looked down. "I couldn't take it. My sister was calling out my name, screaming for me to come and help. I could have saved her and I didn't. I ran. I just ran. I couldn't take hearing her call for me."

"Man..." I trailed off.

"I know, I'm a coward, you don't need to say it."

I shook my head. "I don't think you're a coward. We've all lost people. None of us were prepared for this."

"Did you run? I mean. Leave anyone behind?" he asked.

I thought of Matt. There was nothing I could do for him. I didn't see him get bit and I know it wasn't him that I shot. But I could still see his face. Still hear the sound of his cry in my ears. The fear that had overtaken me. The impulse to survive was overwhelming.

I didn't answer his question.

"Is the place overrun with Z's?"

"No." He wiped his nose of a tear that had fallen. "There are others there. Vile fuckers."

"Like?"

He shook his head. "I don't want talk about. Just trust me. You don't want to drive through there."

I studied his face, trying to gauge if he was lying or not. I didn't get a sense that he was being deceitful. He had experienced something that had shaken him to the core. Perhaps it was just the shock of seeing his family die or maybe it was something far worse.

I slipped back into the truck and for a few seconds I didn't say anything.

"So?" Dax asked.

"Well. We are nearly out of gas. Even if we wanted to go around the town we couldn't. It's the closest town from here."

Izzy leaned over and squinted at the gas gauge.

"We'll be lucky if we even make it there," she said.

"What did he say?" Dax asked inquisitively.

"It doesn't matter, Dax. We just need to be ready. Get in, get some gas, and get out."

Everyone stared at me then looked at Ralphie who was now huddled into a ball on the back of the truck bed.

"Maybe I'll take a turn out there," Specs said. With that he jumped out, Ralphie glanced up, Specs thumbed for him to get in the truck. As we rolled out of Halleck our minds were no longer on gas. We were preoccupied by what was to be found in Wells, Nevada.

TOWN OF THE RISING IDIOTS

We arrived in Wells, Nevada, about an hour after midday. Prior to that we constantly had to swerve our way around more abandoned vehicles. It was like a mass exodus had occurred and no one had made it. By the time we arrived the truck must have been coasting on gas fumes as the needle was in the red.

Wells, like many other small towns in Nevada, looked as if someone had built a wide road through the middle. All the buildings and homes were either side. Ralphie looked nervous as we rolled in.

"Keep your eyes peeled," Dax said.

I checked how much ammo I had left. It wasn't much.

"Ralphie, are there any gun stores in Wells?" Jess asked.

"One, but there's nothing left. They took it."

"Who took it?"

"Never mind."

He returned to gazing out. Ralphie had crunched down in his seat. The windows were tinted but he still looked worried. I pushed open the back window.

"How you doing back there, Specs?"

"Fucking freezing."

"We'll soon get you warmed up."

As we drove down the main street, we all noticed something peculiar. There were no Z's or bodies anywhere.

"I thought you said this place was overrun," Dax piped up.

"It was."

"Why aren't there any Z's?"

"Maybe they wandered off into the desert," Izzy added.

"And took all the dead with them? No, there should be bodies. At least a few."

"Take a left here. The gas station is on the right." Ralphie pointed.

It was beyond strange. We passed by several pristine-looking vans with blacked-out windows as we pulled into the gas station. Not getting out of the truck for a few minutes, we looked around cautiously. Something didn't feel right about the place. It was quiet but nothing had been damaged. No burnt-out cars, no smashed windows.

"How many live here?"

"About thirteen hundred."

Dax was the first one out. "Specs, you give me a hand fueling up. Baja, Johnny, go inside and see what you can scavenge for supplies."

He glanced at Izzy and Jess but they already knew they were to keep an eye on anyone approaching. I stretched my legs and felt my muscles unwind as I got out. I badly needed to take a piss.

Which reminds me. You're probably wondering. How do folks relieve themselves in an apocalypse? No mystery there. Up until that point we just pulled off to the side of the road and went behind a vehicle. One of us would watch out for Z's while the other took care of business. There was no toilet paper so we used old newspaper, rags, or whatever we could find. Anything was better than using our bare hands. Which I might add, surprisingly, newspaper is actually softer than that spiky shit they gave us in high school. Anyway, point made.

Dax and Specs began working on retrieving gas. To their surprise the pump worked.

"How is that possible?"

"Backup generator," Specs said.

"No gas station runs off a generator."

"These must."

Dax raised his eyebrows. He swept the empty street and continued filling up the truck.

* * *

"Something feels really off about this," Baja muttered.

"You're telling me," I said before glancing at Baja

and then realizing he was referring to a dubious-looking sandwich in his hand. We had picked up a stash of food from some of the vehicles but not all of it was edible. Most of it had gone mushy or turned a shade of green. Baja wasn't picky. He continued eating what would have made me throw up. I was just hoping we would find some packages of beef jerky inside.

The bell above the door let out a shrill as we stepped inside. The entire store was in pristine condition. No one had looted it. There wasn't even one item overturned.

"Shit," Baja tossed the half-eaten excuse for a sandwich on the floor and began dashing around the two aisles snatching up packets of chips, candy bars and… he jammed his head under a slushy mixer that was still whirling around. Power? It had to running on a backup generator. I glanced over at the counter expecting to see someone but there was no one there.

"Hello?" I called out.

With a mouthful of slushy he tried to speak. "Oh

you've got to try some of this."

I didn't reply. I was still waiting for a Z to pop out or someone else.

"Oh my god," Baja stared wide-eyed at something on the shelf. "Stop the truck, suck me backwards, and call me Krispin," he uttered before disappearing behind an aisle of shelves and emerging slowly holding a box of Pop-Tarts and some beef jerky in the air like lost treasure.

"I told you. I knew things were on the upswing. This is good, right? It means there's probably more towns like this. You know, ones where the virus hasn't hit." He paused. "Pop-Tarts or jerky?"

"Whatever, I'm gonna take a whiz," I replied, walking slowly out back. Baja opened a bag of beef jerky and started tossing chunks of meat back as though he wouldn't be getting any more for some time.

"Yeah, sure thing, take your time."

I glanced outside the window. Things seemed peaceful. Too peaceful. I hung a left and went down the short corridor. I looked over the photos that hung on the wall. One of them had a certificate and a small picture of a balding man. It read, Tom Knotts, licensed owner.

Where did you go, Tom?

I eased the door that led into the washroom. I peered inside without stepping in. I still had my Glock in hand ready to shoot the first Z that came at me. There had to be some nearby.

It was warm inside. Clean and smelled like bleach as if someone had recently cleaned it up. There were three stalls. Two of them were closed, one was partly open. I readied my gun and kicked the first open. It was empty. I took a deep breath and checked the next. Same again.

"Huh!"

I pushed my handgun back into the holster on my right thigh. I relieved myself, then wandered over to the sink. A quick twist and water gushed out. *Oh, beauty!*

I heaped handfuls over my head and rubbed my face clean. I looked at my reflection in the mirror. I had dark circles beneath my eyes from a lack of sleep. I thought about what it would be like to return to normality. To no longer be worried about Z's. To be able to sleep without the risk of being attacked in the night.

As I dried my hands on a sheet of brown paper towel I peered through a small rectangular window covered in condensation. I could see they had finished fueling up. Specs and Dax were laughing about something. Jess was kneeling in the truck bed, slowly sweeping her assault rifle. Izzy was near the front with Caitlin. Those two had come a long way in a short time. I was worried about Caitlin. She hadn't spoken a word since her sister's death. I was unsure if she would survive the long haul. Death was hard to cope with, but in time you healed. Trauma? None of us knew how to deal with that.

I scanned the street. It was hard to imagine that Wells hadn't been touched by the outbreak. Ralphie said Z's had been here. But where was the evidence? Where was everyone?

I was about to leave the washroom when I caught a glimpse of movement across the street. At first I thought it was my eyes playing tricks on me. With little sleep, and constantly looking for the dead, your eyes started to see things that weren't there. I had already seen my father three times. It was creepy, disturbing, and painful to see.

Of course, it was just my mind replaying events. But it seemed so real.

I came close to the window and looked again. Across the other side of the street was an all-you-could-eat buffet restaurant. The sign above the store read, Black Dragon. I was sure I saw someone beyond the window. Now as I looked there was no one there.

I tossed the crumpled paper towel into the trash and came out. I ducked my head into the small office that was just off to my right. I had hoped to find someone inside. There was no one there either. Nothing had been looted. No drawers overturned. It was if someone had just got up and left. I went in and walked over to the coffee maker. I sniffed it. It was fresh and hot?

Baja was behind the counter scooping boxes of cigarettes into a shopping bag that had on it the words

Thank You For Visiting Wells.

"Dude, you've got to see this."

He reached under the counter and pulled out two handguns. Both had two barrels and two triggers on each of them.

"It fires two bullets at the same time. Have you ever seen anything like this?"

He flipped over one of the handguns. It had two magazines.

"That's some hefty firepower," I replied.

"I can't wait to use this on some Z's." He stashed them inside his flak jacket. I looked around the store while he continued filling up. Specs came to the door.

"How we doing, guys?"

"Specs, get your ass in here. There is tons of food."

"I think Dax wants to get going."

"Tell him to hold onto his panties. There's no rush."

By now Dax was beginning to look nervous. Jess and Izzy were loading up several bottles of water they had found out the front of the store. It almost seemed like a dream. What didn't make sense was that no one else had taken it. The only one that hadn't got out of the truck was Ralphie. I could see him peering out of the window as Dax approached the shop.

He spun his finger in the air. "Wrap it up. We need to shift gears."

"Dax, are you sure? I mean we could hang out here for the night. There seems to be more than enough. What's the hurry?" Izzy asked.

"There's something wrong. I don't like this."

Just as he said that the truck roared to life.

"Hey!" Dax yelled.

Ralphie shot us a wide-eyed look before slamming into gear and burning rubber out of there. Specs lifted his assault rifle and started firing at the truck. Dax followed suit. The back window exploded but he kept going. All of us raced after him. Now I don't know what made us think we were going to catch up but regardless, we kept running.

The truck pulled a hard right and disappeared behind a dark, Gothic-looking building.

"Through here," Dax shouted, spotting a path that cut through the buildings. My chest was burning from running so hard. It didn't help that I kept seeing figures. Were my eyes playing tricks on me again? I would see movement then nothing. As we burst onto the road that the truck had shot down, we were surprised to see the vehicle had stopped in the middle of the road, a few feet from us. It was idling. Ahead, spread across the road, were eight fully armed men. They had formed a human barrier. I mean, it was nothing that the truck couldn't have plowed through, but certainly it was disconcerting. All of them held assault rifles towards the truck, except for one. Panting and out of breath we slowed to a jog and stared at them. They saw us but were focused on Ralphie.

Ralphie slammed the truck into reverse and spun it around. Dax and I didn't wait for him to peel away; we ran at the truck and leapt into the back. Dax had his gun jammed through the back window before Ralphie had a chance to gain speed. Seconds later Dax was holding the keys. Ralphie put his hands in the air.

"You don't understand. We need to get out of here. Those people are going to kill us."

"What the hell are you on about?" I asked.

He looked as if he was about to say something when his eyes widened.

I turned back towards the men who were slowly walking towards the vehicle. They weren't dressed in camo gear or anything that might have made you think that they were militants. They wore ordinary clothes. The only difference was they were carrying firearms. Yet we expected to encounter that everywhere we went. People needed to protect themselves. We would have done the same as them. They formed an arc around the backside of the truck.

"Hey there," the tallest one of the group greeted us. He had dark hair, wore a red plaid shirt, jeans, and dark shoes. There was not a speck of dirt on him, or the others for that matter. His eyes darted between us and Ralphie who was now even more panicked.

I had my weapon on the ready. Specs and Baja were the same. Jess and Izzy must have stayed with Caitlin back at the gas station as I couldn't see them.

He raised a hand. "We don't mean any harm." The man lowered his gun. "I see you've helped yourself to supplies."

"Who are you?" I asked.

He shook his head. "Just townsfolk."

"Where are the Z's?"

"The what?"

"The infected?"

"There are none left."

I frowned, trying to make sense of what they were saying

"Don't believe them," Ralphie shouted out.

The man looked past me with a grin. "Good to see you again, brother. We wondered where you had gone."

Brother?

I looked at both of them trying to see a

resemblance. I couldn't see it.

Dax cast a glance at the other men who still had their guns fixed on us. We could feel the tension and expected the worst.

"I'm Isaac," he said, stepping forward and extending his hand. We just looked at it. We were in no mood for shaking hands. "I understand. I know how this must look." He told the others to relax. They lowered their weapons but kept a firm grip on them.

"Where are the other people in the town?"

"In city hall." He turned and pointed to an old-fashioned church with a large steeple. The double wooden doors were open and several others looked on. "We have a meeting at noon each day."

"And you leave this place wide open? No guards?"

He let out a short laugh. "Oh we don't have anything to fear."

"Don't listen to him."

"Come on, Ralphie, is that anyway to treat a brother?"

"You are no brother of mine."

"Listen, we just wanted to get a few things and be on our way," Dax said.

"By all means. We aren't going to stop you. However, we would like it if you would join us this evening for a meal."

"No," Ralphie yelled.

Dax cleared his throat. "Um. Thanks but we need to get going."

"Ah, that's a shame," Isaac replied.

Baja tapped me on the arm. "Maybe we should. I mean, we have basically robbed them of all their supplies."

He overheard Baja. "You haven't robbed us. It's yours to take."

I looked at Dax to see what he wanted to do. Meanwhile others were coming out of the church. They were older. They didn't appear to pose a threat. Some were in their late forties, others their sixties. By all accounts they looked like regular townspeople. There was nothing that made me think they were anything more than a town that may have managed to get things under control. It was possible. Just because Castle Rock went to shit so fast, it didn't mean every other town had. Maybe they quarantined those who were bit?

"What do you think?" Baja asked.

I turned to Dax and whispered, "If they wanted to kill us, I think they would have attacked now, right?"

He nodded.

"What about Ralphie?" he asked.

We cast a glance over at him. He was hunched behind the wheel looking as if he was about to bolt.

"Maybe. Maybe we can stay, just for a meal," Dax replied to Isaac.

"Just for a meal. Superb," Isaac said. "Come, I'll introduce you to some of the others."

I could hear Ralphie muttering to himself. "No. No."

We didn't know what to make of Ralphie. There was something he wasn't telling us. Besides the odd behavior, the place seemed normal enough. Though I was still guarded, something didn't feel right. I asked Specs to go get Jess and the others.

"Oh, don't worry. We will have someone pick up your other friends."

Specs looked back at me. I shrugged.

THE DAMNED

It was an unusual gathering. They had requested that our weapons remain at the door, which gave us even more reason to feel uneasy. When asked why, Isaac told us that they had a zero policy about weapons inside the house of the Lord. They promised the weapons would still be there when we left. We were reluctant at first. After talking among ourselves and getting a whiff of the hot food, our stomachs made the final decision. I wasn't sure what Ralphie's issue was with these people. Sure, eating a meal in a church was a little odd, but they appeared to act pretty darn normal.

"So you were saying that you were from Castle Rock? The mining town?" one of them said in between drinks of orange juice.

"Yeah, that's it."

He nodded. They had set out a large mahogany table in the church. It extended from the door all the way down to the other end. At the far end was a stained-glass window with a depiction of the cross.

"Not many people there, I imagine?" he asked.

"About the same as here. Which by the way, where are the others?"

As we waited for our food, we learned that when the virus hit their town many of the community had died, but a small number of them had managed to get it under control. They had salvaged what they could. Burned the dead and were in the process of rebuilding the town.

Across the table one of the men sneered at me.

There was something about meeting strangers. The way they look at you as if they are judging you. I didn't like it one bit. The interaction with them reminded me of when I was a kid and our parents took us to visit our aunties and uncles out in West Virginia. It was awkward. We had to bunk with our cousins who we had never seen before. They were all hicks. Living out in the backwoods, eating off the land, and spending most of the time up to their knees in cow shit.

"Are you all that remains?" Isaac asked.

"As far as we know. I don't think many people had a chance to escape. It happened too quickly."

He nodded and glanced at one of the other men who was standing by the door.

"Why haven't you blocked off the roads?" I asked. "You know, to prevent Z's from showing up on your doorstep?"

"The Lord watches over us."

It was then I noticed that each of them wore a gold ring. Like the kind given out to those who had made it through police academy or a group that was part of a secret society.

"You always lived here?" I asked.

"No. Some of us came in from out of town looking for supplies. I was from the city but when things got bad, we decided to find somewhere we could start again."

"And you settled on Wells?"

He took another sip of his drink as two women wheeled a trolley out that had cooked meat, potatoes, and vegetables on it.

"Wells is small. Simple. Exactly what we need."

I looked over at Ralphie. His eyes were down, occasionally he would glance up.

"How do you know Ralphie?" Dax asked.

"We are brothers."

"Brothers? But he said his brother died."

"Oh, not by blood. Brothers in the Lord. Which by the way, I must thank you for bringing him back to us. We were very concerned for him. We had no idea where he'd gone."

I nodded slowly. "Not a problem, but I don't think he plans on staying."

"He'll stay," Isaac said it with full confidence.

They began dishing up food. My stomach was grumbling. There were about thirty of us in the hall. A few men stood by the doors, occasionally glancing out as if they were expecting trouble. Isaac sat directly to my right. Another man to the side of me leaned in and asked, "Tell me. Are the three females virgins?"

I nearly spat my orange juice out. "What?" I stammered.

"Pure."

I frowned. "What the hell does that have to do with anything?"

The volume of discussion around the table was loud enough that only Isaac and I heard.

"Joseph," Isaac gave him a look of death. "Excuse our brother for being so forthright. In this age it's rare to find those who are pure. He's just curious."

I wasn't sure how to reply to that. His comment wasn't just unusual, it was downright creepy. I looked over at Jess, relieved she hadn't heard, otherwise the guy might have found himself chewing on a bullet.

Two young children came by and handed us each a plate of food. I stared down at it as steam spiraled up. The smell made my stomach rumble.

"Looks good."

"It's been a while since we've had a hot meal," Dax said.

I was about to tuck into it when Isaac coughed. I glanced at him with my fork just about to enter my mouth. The others around the table glared. I placed my fork down.

"Sister Rachael, perhaps you would like to give thanks."

She gave a nod before closing her eyes and bowing. It was your typical prayer. Now I can't begin to say how uncomfortable this made me feel. I had grown up in a household where no one ever prayed over their food. We had a stretch or starve mentality. About the only thing my father was thankful for was the fridge stocked with beer.

When the woman was done we began to eat. The cutlery clattered as discussion continued.

"Tell me, Johnny, are you a believer?" Isaac asked.

I took a bite of a potato.

"I never really had a need."

"Everyone has a need."

I began to feel a little warm around the collar. I knew wars had been started over what people believed. We were guests, our weapons were in a box by the door. I certainly didn't want to offend the man. They had been kind enough to invite us for a meal. Even though they were a little strange, it made a change to meet someone who wasn't out to slit our throats. I thought back to the small group we had met at the motel.

"Not eating, brother?" Isaac asked.

Specs chuckled to himself. I had a rough feeling what he was snickering about. He'd always found the mention of brotherhood, funny. He had once thrown a bunch of firecrackers into the local parish church just so he could see the pastor swear. For weeks he had been telling us that the guy swore but none of us bought it. The guy was as clean as a whistle. Every interaction with him was like greeting an angel. Specs was determined to prove it. That's when the firecrackers were brought in. He hadn't told us what he had planned that night and by the time we figured it out, it was too late.

The pastor came out of his house, dropping f-bombs as if he thought it was World War Three.

"This tastes a little funky but it's not bad," Baja said, shoveling another load of meat into his mouth.

Baja, ah, he tended to not give a rat's ass what anyone believed. He tossed around curse words like they were going out of fashion.

I looked over at Ralphie. He looked down at his meal with disgust, his eyes flicked around the room. He shook his head.

"Come now. It will give you sustenance, brother."

"I'm not your brother."

Isaac's lip curled up. I hadn't tasted the meat yet. I brought a piece up to my mouth. "You have livestock left?" I asked.

"It's frozen, leftovers since the outbreak."

"Lucky." I was always one for a good steak. As I placed it in my mouth Ralphie was shaking his head slowly. I frowned as I began to chew.

His eyes widened and then he came out with it.

"Don't swallow. It's human."

I was in mid-chew when he said that. Our eyes fixed on each other. A chunk of chewed-up meat rolled out of Baja's lips onto his plate. Isaac appeared to pay no attention. He continued eating his with little regard for what Ralphie had just blurted out. I placed my knife and fork down.

"Problem?" Isaac asked.

"What is this meat?" Dax asked.

"Poultry."

"Don't believe him. He keeps them below the barn."

"Keeps what?" Specs asked.

"Ralphie, you do have a wild imagination. Perhaps that's why you ran."

"I ran because you killed my brother."

"But didn't you say your father did that?"

I didn't know what to believe anymore. Ralphie got up and tried to leave but one of the men got in front of him.

"Get out of the way, Peter."

"Ralphie, please, come sit down," Isaac said. "You are being rude."

Dax wasn't liking this. Neither were we, especially since our weapons were out of reach. One by one we dropped cutlery onto the plates. Isaac wiped his mouth and tossed his rag down.

"Now I try to be nice. Give you a meal and —"

"I think it's time we leave," Dax said cutting him off.

Isaac gave a nod to two of his men and they pulled their assault rifles up. We might as well have been caught with our pants around our ankles. I pressed my back against the table and took a hold of a knife without anyone seeing. I slipped it up my sleeve just as several more of his men moved in and grabbed each of us. We tried to resist but there were too many. We were thrown to the ground and zip-tied. With our hands behind our backs they marched us out of the hall and led us down the street. It was getting dark outside. Snow was coming down heavy. This had all been a bad idea, but how were we to know? Yes, everyone was a potential threat but they hadn't kicked up a fuss until Ralphie spoke out. And what, were we meant to believe someone who had tried to steal our truck? What was his deal anyway? Who were these people? I had questions that needed answers but right now I just wanted to know where we were going.

"Put them in the store for now. We'll deal with them later."

They led us up to a store that had blacked-out windows. No lights were on outside so I couldn't see the name of the store, however, I knew the second they tossed us inside what it was. The light from outside reflected off a few tall objects.

It was a sex shop. Baja burst out laughing. "Anyone fancy a fuck before we die?" he said.

"Oh shut up," Izzy said.

Each of us found a place. Specs leaned up against the counter. Izzy, Jess, and Caitlin sat on the floor. Dax immediately went into military mode and started looking for anything that could get us out of our zip ties. I just waited until they shut the door before I pulled out the knife and squeezed it between my palms.

"Anyone want to give me a hand?"

"No, but I'm sure there's a toy for that," Baja muttered as he glanced at the various packaged gadgets lined up on shelves.

Jess jumped up, she turned her back and took a hold of the knife and then started to move it back and forth. It was tough as it was only a butter knife and the zip ties were made of a thick plastic. Though within a matter of about five minutes she had managed to cut through. I rubbed my wrists and did the same for the others. However, it was a little easier this time.

Ralphie sat quietly in the corner. I think he knew what was about to happen. As soon as Dax was out of his restraints he had Ralphie up against the wall.

"You knew damn well what you were leading us into."

"I told you to go around. But you wouldn't listen

to me."

"Start talking. Who are these people? What do they want?" Dax hollered.

"And more importantly, was that really human flesh?" Specs asked.

"Alright I see you have that handled. I'm going to look for weapons while you guys work it out." Baja strolled off into the darkness of the store.

"Are you even from this town?" Jess asked.

"Yes. But they're not."

"So what happened?" I asked.

"They were already here when the outbreak kicked off. That's when they shot a cop and took over."

"Why didn't you tell us?"

"They…" he stuttered.

"Spit it out, man." Dax was getting angrier by the second.

"They have my sister."

There was silence.

"The one you said was dead?" I asked.

"I had two. One of them my father killed, the other was taken by them."

"Who are they?"

"Some cult. I don't know what it is they believe. I remember them being in the town. They kept to themselves. I didn't know they were messed up in the head. I just thought they were another religion. Heck, I believe but not what they do."

Dax still had a tight grip on him. His jacket was pushed right up to his face.

"Ease off, Dax," I said. "Dax, let him go."

"And the meat?" Specs asked.

"Human flesh. Zombie flesh? How else do you think they can survive out here?"

Jess doubled over. "Oh god, I think I'm gonna be sick."

"So the whole gas station is just a ploy to lure people in?"

He nodded. "Listen, guys, I would never purposely try to harm you."

"Shut up," Dax added.

We stood there in the dark contemplating our next move.

"We need to get out of here. Get our weapons."

"Speaking of weapons, I think I found some," Baja said coming out the back waving around two thirteen-inch dildos. Specs palmed his own forehead.

"No, I'm serious. Add the cords from those vagina balls over there and I could make myself a mean pair of nunchucks. And fuck 'em up real good. No pun intended."

"Baja. This is not the time."

But it was too late. Waving them around, he lost his grip on one of them and it hit Izzy in the face. "Oh shit," he muttered.

"Oh shit, indeed, Baja, I'm going to ram this up your ass."

We continued to get more information from Ralphie while Izzy chased Baja around the store, wielding an oversized lifelike cock.

"Why the hell are they eating humans?" Jess asked.

"They see this whole thing as a gift from their god. Z's killing humans. Another form of manna from heaven."

"Ah man, why do we always have to meet the freaks?" Specs said, taking a peek outside the blinds to see if anyone was coming.

"I would have told you sooner but my sister..."

"So you did leave behind your sister?" I asked.

"I had no choice. They would have killed me too."

Ralphie slumped down on the floor, tears began to roll down his cheeks.

"What now?" Jess asked.

"We need to get the guns, the truck, and get the hell out of freakville," Dax said, already looking like he was about to charge out of there.

"Easier said than done."

I wandered up and down the aisles trying to think. "There has to be a back entrance to this place."

"Oh, there's a back entrance." Baja snorted as he

rushed by.

"Yeah, and I'm about to find it," Izzy hollered. Now most might have told them to settle down while we tried to figure this out. But we were so used to their demented antics it just became background noise — at least to me.

"Sit the fuck down," Dax had reached his breaking point. I rarely saw him like that but when he was, you did what he said or found a good place to hide. Baja and Izzy scuffed their feet, swapping "we'll settle this later" glances.

"How does this work?" I asked Ralphie.

"What do you mean?"

"Do they wait until you're bitten before they use you for chow?"

"No. They feed you to those ugly bastards. Hell, they worship them."

"What?" I stammered, unable to hide my disgust.

He moved over to the windows and pulled the blinds down. "You see that barn up there. Inside that is a hole. Everyone who has already turned is down there.

They lower people down into it. They have this whole ritual that they do. It's sick."

"Dead, though?"

"No, alive. They lower people down alive. My brother broke his arm when this whole thing kicked off. Instead of letting him live, they lowered him down and let those flesh-eating monsters tear him apart. They do it just enough until they are dead, and then raise them back up. Before they turn they strip them of the flesh. That's what you were eating."

"Holy fuck."

It was hard to imagine, but then again, there had been cults that had done far worse things to people even when there was no apocalypse.

"When do they do this?"

"As soon as they need more food. Who knows. Maybe tonight. Perhaps tomorrow. But we are going to end up on a plate."

"Not if I have anything to say about it," Dax replied.

DEATH BY DILDO

As much as I didn't like it, we had few options. Stripped of our weapons, we would now be stripped of our dignity. Like a scene from a badly filmed low-budget porno, we stood there kitted out in gear that would have made even a porn star blush.

Like any good battalion readying themselves for battle we had spent the past twenty minutes going up and down the aisles grabbing anything that could be used as a weapon. Trust me, I didn't like it any better than anyone else. Though, Baja thought it was great that we had finally come to our senses and were listening to him.

Now hold on.

It wasn't the case that we were actually following his bright idea, it's just that we had exhausted all our other options. We ran through all manner of ideas as the hours passed. One of which was making a run back to city hall and hoping that they had the box of weapons still there, another was attacking them in their sleep. All of which meant exposing ourselves to risk, and all of them required us getting out first.

And getting out was the challenge. You see at that precise moment they were under the assumption that we were secured and locked up in the den of iniquity. The plan was to have the girls seated with their hands behind their backs to give the illusion that we were still tied. Baja wanted to vote on having Izzy and Jess fully naked to create more of a distraction.

Don't worry; he eventually recovered from the kick to his nuts after coming up with that idea.

The floor in front of the door would be covered in massage oil.

I know. It sounds like a gag you would see in an episode of Wile E. Coyote and the Road Runner. But, seriously that stuff was as slippery as shit. After seeing how well it worked, I had tried to coerce Jess into giving me a back rub with it. But she just slapped me.

Now I would like to say that it was a good idea, but it was actually the result of an accident. Ralphie had toppled over a stack of the glass bottles. That's the only reason there was a big bloody pool of the stuff spread out like a mini pond. The shattered glass was just an added bonus.

Baja stared down at the arsenal of weapons attached around his waist. "I swear this is some serious A-Team shit. Not even Hannibal could have come up with this."

"I feel like a real dick," Specs said.

"You look like one," Dax replied.

There we were, ready to take on two or more heavily armed men with little more than a large selection of various sized dildos and Ben Wa steel balls. Now I know what you're thinking. We were out of our minds? Look, to be fair we could have beaten them to death with a whole host of items on the shelves because there were lots of paddles, whips, chains, and various indigestible spiky items that looked as if they could do some serious damage. Why anyone would buy something like that for pleasure, though, was beyond me. But — each to their own.

The upside was, if we did manage to lure them into our asinine plan, and overcome them, we had plenty of rope and gag balls to keep them quiet.

"How did you guys talk me into this?" Ralphie asked.

I stood back to take a look at them all. I could barely keep myself together.

Besides the makeshift nunchucks that Baja insisted he make, he was sporting a black latex mask with a zipper for his mouth. Why? I'm still trying to figure that out.

Specs, he was protesting as to why he had to wear nipple clamps. Jess told him they looked threatening. Really, there was no reason, other than the fact we were all getting a kick out of it.

As for Ralphie, he just looked on as if he had entered an episode of *The Twilight Zone*.

Dax stood off to one side. There was no way on

God's green earth that he was going to touch any of that shit. Now I would like to say that was it, but just for added measure, Jess had armed Ralphie, Specs, and Baja with three hard black paddles. Each one had glow-in-the-dark words engraved on it. Ralphie's said SLUT, Specs's was SLAVE, and Baja was BITCH.

After seeing that I nearly lost it.

"Right, so everyone knows the plan. Let's get to it," Dax said, shaking his head in disbelief.

With no power, and the only light coming in from the moon outside, it offered the perfect amount of cover. They had positioned two men on the outside. Ralphie's job was to try and convince them that he had information Isaac would want to know. He banged on the door. The men obviously had strict instructions not to open the door so they didn't respond initially. That's when it was proposed that I would start a fight with Ralphie. Of course we still had to pretend that our hands were tied. I began shoving Ralphie hard into the glass door.

"Keep that up, we'll put a round in you," one of the

men said from the other side.

"You don't understand, he's trying to kill me. For the love of God and all things holy, help me."

They weren't stupid. When they cracked the door they didn't rush in. They had small lights on the end of their assault rifles. As much as I found our plan amusing, this was deadly serious. One bullet was all it would take and it would be lights out. At the sound of the door creaking open we rushed back into the darkness of the room. The noise of our struggle was loud as we charged into aisles knocking over anything that wasn't nailed down.

Their gun barrels swept around trying to pinpoint us as we moved back and forth. They had to enter if they wanted to get a better look at where all of us were positioned.

"Get on the floor. Now," they yelled.

We ignored their commands and I pushed Ralphie into an aisle that was just out of view of the doorway. It was enough to make them think they could stop it. That's when they ran inside. What happened next occurred fast.

Besides them slipping on the pool of oil.

Dax, Specs, and Baja had been either side of the doorway crouched down. The attack was fast, vicious, and I have to admit, downright sexy. It was only after I found out what the three of them had done that I laughed. Initially they didn't attack the men; instead, they knocked the assault rifles out of their hands. After that they paddled and slapped them into submission. In many ways I was kind of glad I couldn't see what was going on, as I was pretty sure I would have been in fits of laughter.

Izzy and Jess tied them up and put gag balls in their mouths. We tossed the rest of the ridiculous-looking items in a pile and snatched up the two assault rifles, three mags each, and a couple of Walther P22s.

"Now this what I call a weapon!" Dax looked happy again.

Dax snatched up a bag that he must have put together earlier. Glass rattled inside it. I had no idea what he had in mind but I knew we didn't have long. We had been stuck inside that store for over four hours. It was just after two in the morning when we got out. Baja came out a few minutes after.

"What were you doing?"

"Just some final touches." He smirked. I didn't even want to know.

First order of business was finding the truck. The worst-case scenario we would have to hot-wire it. We needed our weapons back but we had already been low on ammo when they had taken them from us. Somehow I could tell Dax wasn't ready to just bolt. The look on his face said it all. He had vengeance on his mind.

"Where do they stay?" Dax asked.

"Uh," Ralphie replied.

Dax had his game face on. "Speak up."

"The two houses." He pointed towards the barn. "The farmhouses are close by, one beside the large barn and another is one field over."

"They all live together?"

Ralphie shrugged. "That's just what I remember."

"Jess, Izzy, Specs, head over to city hall see if you can collect the weapons. Take Ralphie with you. If you find the truck, swing it around. Keep the lights off. Wait for us at the bottom of this street. Be ready to go."

"What about my sister?" Ralphie asked.

"Do you know for sure that she's still alive?" I asked.

"We are not going to risk any more lives," Dax spat out.

"I don't know. But I have to see."

"Oh, you run from this town, and leave her behind and now you grow a fucking conscience?" Dax asked.

Ralphie shrugged. Dax shook his head in frustration. I could imagine what he was thinking when he looked at me. He probably thought I was going to give him heck if we didn't at least try to find the girl.

"Alright, you come with us."

Under the cover of night, we moved across the street and down a back alley. We could hear moaning. It was getting louder. No doubt coming from the barn.

Ralphie led the way. It took us close to ten minutes to make it to a street that led up to the first farmhouse. The barn was a football field away. It was up on a steep hill overlooking the town. At night it looked ominous. Only the glow from the moon revealed its blood-red color. We could hear the sound of a few Z's shuffling along in the forest. We waited until the coast was clear before we hopped over a fence and began our ascent to the barn. I had to hope that the others were okay.

When we made it to the barn door, we paused, glancing up at the house.

"This is a bad idea," Dax said.

Ralphie unhooked the latch and opened the huge barn door. Dust and small pieces of hay filled the air. Inside the smell of horse shit permeated everything. That and the smell of death. The sound of moaning was loud but we couldn't see shit.

It was like any typical two-story barn. Down either side were empty stables. Most of them were filled with haystacks. The sound of moaning was loud. It was pitch-black inside. We had only taken a few steps when Ralphie yanked us back. It was lucky we hadn't gone any further. Dax turned on the small flashlight on the end of the assault rifle. He lowered it to the floor and then our eyes widened. In front of our feet was a giant sinkhole that went the full length of the barn. We were standing right at the edge. One more step and I would have fallen into a pit of snarling Z's. There had to be over two hundred gnashing their teeth. Among them were fresh dead, their bodies barely decayed. No doubt they'd been killed that night. Most of the dead were missing body parts. Jaws hanging loose, stomachs torn out, and blood gushing from their mouths.

"Holy shit, they need a makeover," Baja said.

Dax swept the light over their faces.

"Do you see her?"

"She's not down there," he said. Ralphie just stared down, mesmerized by the Z's.

Caitlin remained silent.

"What do you think?" I asked Dax.

"Everyone out." He grabbed hold of me. "Johnny, take Ralphie and Baja up to the house. Caitlin can stay with me. See if you can spot his sister. Don't go in. The first sign of trouble you get out of there." Dax tossed me his assault rifle.

"Roger that. What are you doing to do?"

"Just go. I'll follow in a moment."

I led the way. I turned back briefly to see Dax taking out of a bag a large glass bottle of massage oil from the store. *What the fuck?* I knew he was a kinky bastard but offering a full body massage to a Z? I shook my head and kept running towards the house.

"Dude, we're never going to find her in there," Baja said. "She's probably doggy chow by now."

"Shut the hell up!" Ralphie shot back.

We were just getting close to the house when a few bullets snapped past our heads. That was followed by floodlights turning on. No doubt powered by a generator. Immediately after the sound of a tornado siren began. It was so loud we could barely hear ourselves think.

"You think they could have bought a louder one?" Baja laughed, turning around and bolting.

I yanked Ralphie's arm. "Let's go."

"No, my sister."

"It's not happening, man. I'm sorry."

"Ralphie," The faint sound of a girl's scream cut into the noise.

Ralphie looked back, his eyes widened, and his jaw dropped. "There she is."

Isaac was standing outside the house. With the floodlight on we could see him clearly. He had a knife up to her throat. The siren turned off.

"I told you what I would do if you ran again."

Ralphie's eyes bulged in his head. Then, without missing a beat Isaac sliced the girl from ear to ear, blood gushed, and she dropped to his feet.

"NO!" Ralphie screamed. Isaac licked his hand that was covered in blood.

I grabbed a hold of Ralphie, but he pulled back. "Get off."

Before I had time to think he'd grabbed the assault rifle from me and began firing wildly at the house.

"Johnny. Let's go." Dax was a short distance from the barn. A trail of fire was making its way towards it. I turned back and grabbed Ralphie with both hands yanking him back. He was resisting but I think he knew that there was little we could do now. There were far more of them than us. The light in the second farmhouse went on and men were pouring out with weapons.

"Move it." I pushed him forward. My legs and chest were killing me. We jumped over the line of fire that was snaking its way to the barn. Bullets were snapping as we returned fire all the while running into the darkness of the night, hoping that it would offer cover.

As we were rushing down the hill, we saw more Z's coming out of the tree line. A few of the fast ones took some of their people down. Now their fight was with the dead.

A pair of lights flashed on. We heard the rumble of the engine. The others had found the truck. It was stationed just at the edge of the road, idling. The door swung open, the interior light inside illuminated Jess and the rest. Right then behind us was a mighty explosion. An inferno raged and a fireball flew up into the air. It was followed by an even bigger one. I looked back for a second and saw those attempting to put out the fire were being overrun by Z's coming out of the forest.

We hopped the fence and dived into the truck. The back wheels spun wildly in the mud as Izzy gunned it out of there. It was only when we were a short distance down the street that our stomachs sank.

"Did you get the weapons?" Dax asked.

"No. We checked inside," Specs replied. "They were gone."

"Great, so all we have is two handguns, two assault rifles, and minimal ammo."

"We still have a dildo!" Baja said, lifting it in the air like the sword of King Arthur.

"Oh my god," I shook my head in disbelief.

"Where's Caitlin?" Dax shouted.

Izzy slammed the brakes on. I jumped out followed by Baja and Specs.

"Caitlin! Caitlin." One by one we shouted at the top of our voices into the darkness.

"I'm here." We spun around. I breathed a sigh of relief. She had dived into the back of the truck. And there was me thinking she had lost all sense of reality. She was tuned into what was going on probably more than we were. I helped her out and we hopped back into the truck. The reflection of fire in our side mirrors flickered as we peeled out of the town that would no doubt haunt us for a long time.

GRAFFITI CITY

It had been two days since we had lost Millie. Caitlin had been silent the whole time until she spoke those words. She was in an almost comatose state. Staring out of the window, I followed her gaze, wondering what she was seeing. Beyond the glass was nothing except a desolate horizon of fire and smoke.

It was just after dawn when we arrived in the city. We passed signs for the airport. It had taken us the better part of eight days from Castle Rock to Salt Lake City. A hellish drive that I wouldn't care to repeat. We had abandoned the truck three miles from the city limits because there was no way of getting in. It almost appeared as if someone had purposely blocked off the highway. Three semi-trailers from the back of trucks were positioned sideways, smaller cars were jammed beneath.

We were low on ammo and supplies. All of us were hopeful that we would find what we needed in the city.

It was strange to see the concrete jungle so quiet. Dax and I had only ever once visited Salt Lake City when I was around the age of eight. It was a stark contrast to the way I remembered it. Steel and concrete towered over us, bordered by the Great Salt Lake and the snow-capped peaks of the Wasatch Mountain Range. Built back in 1847 by the Mormons, it had grown into a diverse city. Boasting of some of the best ski resorts in the United States.

We had no idea what we were walking into, only that we needed to locate where the radio message was being broadcast. I guess we expected to find military on scene, as there were two military bases in Utah. Hill Air Force Base, thirty miles away, and Fort Douglas which was three miles from the city. But we saw no military personnel.

"Seems a little too quiet," Specs said as we trudged our way in. Ralphie hadn't spoken a word since his sister's death. There was no way to cherry-coat it. By the time this would be over we were all certain we would lose more.

"Just keep your wits about you," I said.

Sheets of paper blew across the streets like tumbleweed. Signs of the military making one last stand could be seen as we passed a burnt-out helicopter among an ocean of Humvees, tanks, barricades, and machine guns emptied of bullets. Everywhere we turned windows had been blown out or cracked. The walls were plastered in graffiti. Red, blue, green, and purple. It was if someone had gone crazy with a spray can.

I stared up at the dark windows. A sense that someone was watching was prevalent. It wasn't the death and destruction that was all around that bothered me, as much as it was the bodies hanging from lampposts like piñatas. Most of them were military; others were dressed in business attire. Every street had them. We must have counted at least forty. In other areas there were heads that had been decapitated and shoved down on top of parking meters like popsicles. Someone was definitely sending out a clear message. But who would do this?

Food was the only thing racing through our minds. After the little we had scavenged from the town of the rising idiots, we were ready to stock back up. Baja was grumbling about his gut, and I could have used something decent to eat. In the city there was far more choice than we could ever hope to find. Though most of the stores and restaurants that weren't already looted had metal security shutters pulled down. Jess spotted a sign for City Creek Center but it would have taken us hours to get there by foot. We saw a small, partially enclosed market square. The first store was a whole food place and the only one that didn't look overrun with Z's. Though we figured some of those creepy bastards would be inside.

"Shit, can't we go in that kebab shop?" Baja asked.

"After what we just went through, I don't want to see another piece of cooked meat," Izzy replied.

"You are aware that just because they sell whole foods, they do sell lean meats," Specs added.

Izzy just rolled her eyes. Like most of the stores the windows had been smashed in as people either tried to escape or break in. We would have pulled our knives but we didn't have any. The plan was simple. Baja, Ralphie, and Specs would take on any Z's lingering outside while Jess, Izzy, and Caitlin went in. They would then follow after them. Dax and I were going to see if we could find anything in the next store called Wilderness Outfitters. It sold hunting, fishing, and camping gear. The first order of business was to get some camping stoves, after that it was anything that could be used as a weapon. We watched as the girls stepped over broken glass and waded their way through the window display.

"You guys good?" Dax asked.

"We got this."

"Remember, don't start firing unless you have to. Keep an eye on the girls," I told Specs.

"Um, I think we can handle ourselves," Izzy muttered.

Dax and I had nothing to use for weapons. We

crouched low and slid underneath a partially closed rolling shutter. It was dark inside. We had taken one of the flashlights off the one assault rifle. Dax swept the light across the tops of the merchandise. I stamped my foot on the ground and we waited to see if anything showed up. Nothing. We pressed in further.

"We need more light in here. Go roll up the shutters just a little," he ordered.

As I moved back towards the shutters I heard something whip past my head. It was an arrow. It embedded itself in the wall. My heartbeat started racing.

"Don't you dare lift that," a voice came from the darkness.

I spun around scanning the area. "Who are you? Show yourself."

"What are you doing in my store?"

Dax looked at me and motioned for me to go one way while he went the other.

We lowered ourselves down until the darkness enveloped us. On the floor I looked beneath the stands of goods trying to see if I could spot anyone. It was too dark.

"We just need a few supplies then we'll be on our way."

"You got money?" the gruff voice asked.

"Are you serious?" Dax replied.

"You want something, you pay for it."

"Have you had your head under a rock? Society has collapsed. There is no monetary system," I said.

"There is in my world," the voice replied. I was the closest to the voice. I still couldn't see him; all I could do was slowly move forward, hoping to catch a glimpse of our mystery man.

"It's over. The world has to gone to shits," I said.

"Maybe. But I still own this place."

I crept closer. I could hear his voice coming from just over the counter where the register was. I was down on my hands and knees and crawling along being ever so careful to not make any noise. I was just closing in on the counter when I felt something sharp, cold, and hard pressed against my temple.

"That's right. Slowly does it."

I rose to my feet, flashing a sideways glance to get a better look at who this was. In the darkness I could make out what he was holding to my head. It was an archery bow.

"You can come out as well. I know you are over there."

The silhouette of Dax's head popped up a few feet away.

"Listen, we don't want any trouble. We are just out of supplies. We had our own weapons but they were taken from us."

"Too bad. Let me guess, you haven't eaten in a while either."

"No," I replied.

"How do I know I can trust you?"

"Well, other than the fact we have no weapons," I said.

"That's not what I saw."

I hesitated before I replied, "Oh you mean our

friends?"

"That's who they are?"

"Yeah, they are searching for food from next door."

"Really?" he replied. I caught an edge to his voice.

There was a long pause.

"You don't own that place too, do you?"

He nodded.

"Shit," I replied.

Then as quickly as he had placed the arrow against my head he removed it.

"Go tell your friends to come on inside."

I cast a glance at Dax.

"Well, go on," he said.

Dax backed up slowly.

I heard the sound of metal turning, then a light came on. It was a hand-crank flashlight. The light illuminated his face. He looked Hispanic but it was hard to tell in the dim light. Possibly in his early thirties? He wore black tactical gear, everything was black.

"Where have you come from?" he asked.

"Castle Rock."

He snorted. "That's quite a distance. Why are you here?"

"We heard a signal being broadcast. There is meant to be some safe zones. Do you know anything about that?"

"Nope."

"What's your name?" I asked.

"Benjamin. Benjamin Garcia."

"I'm Johnny."

Behind me the others came traipsing in. I turned to see Dax carrying Caitlin. He was hurrying.

"What happened?" I yelled.

"She's been bit."

SWAT

"Bring her through here," Benjamin said. He led us around the back of the store and behind a makeshift fake wall that he had set up in front of some stairs. At the top of the stairwell he led us into a room that was completely blacked out.

"Place her here."

He swept his hand across a large table. Cutlery, plates, and cups fell on the floor. Among them was a map.

"Over in the corner are some lights, you'll need to crank them to get them going."

A few minutes passed. It was easier to see him now. I turned my attention to Caitlin who had a huge chunk taken out of her forearm. The bone was exposed and flesh was dangling down like a stuck-out tongue. She was out cold.

"We're going to need to amputate it," Benjamin said, grabbing up some towels.

"We can save her?" Jess asked.

He glanced at her. "There's no guarantee."

"So the virus hasn't entered her bloodstream?"

He laughed.

"What's funny?" I asked.

"You don't need to get bit to have the virus. You already have it."

"What?"

"That's why the dead are walking. I don't know the logistics of it. But if you die, you become one of them. Surely you must have seen that by now?"

I frowned. "I don't get it?"

Caitlin gasped, her eyelids fluttered. Izzy came close and began to hold her head.

"Where am I?" There was fear in her eyes and voice.

"Listen, I'm not a doctor. All I know is that if you die, you turn. If you get bit, you will turn eventually.

Maybe scratches and bites speed up the process of transformation. If we cut the arm now, she has a fifty-fifty chance of survival."

"No," she stammered. "I don't want you to cut it."

"It's okay, Caitlin. He's trying to help," Izzy added.

"No, you don't understand. I just want to die."

"But we could save you," Jess said, coming close to her and gripping her hand.

She was breathing hard, trying to find words. "I just want to be with my sister. I can't take this anymore. I've lost everyone."

We looked at each other, unsure of what to do or say.

Listening to her talk about her family reminded me of my own. In many ways I was glad my mother didn't live long enough to see all this happen. I was grateful that the connection to my father was shallow. If a person was to survive in this new world, they couldn't hold tightly to those around them. Or was that the key to survival?

I knew one day I might lose Dax. What then?

Would I fall to pieces? Would I be unable to find the will to live? Was it even worth living? There were so many questions, and few answers that satisfied. After what we had witnessed on our way to the city, there had been a few brief moments when I was tempted to put a gun to my own head and end it. After all the atrocities we had seen, and those we were yet to see. Was the quality of life worth fighting for?

Jess looked to us for an answer. As if somehow we could convince Caitlin that life was worth living. The truth was, all of us had been stripped of hope. We had seen more horrors in the past week than we had in all the years we had been alive. Images of death, depravity, and pain filled every crevice of our minds.

"Caitlin, is this really what you want?" I asked. She nodded, affirmatively.

Jess grabbed hold of me and dragged me to one side.

"Are you really going to give up on her?"

"Jess, it's not for us to decide. It's her life."

"That's bullshit. Would you let me go?"

I stared blankly at her. "No."

"Then convince her not to do this."

I shook my head. "It's not that easy."

"Yes it is. You make a choice for another person. You think about them instead of yourself."

"What? You don't think I want her to survive?"

She studied my face before walking away.

"How long before I turn?" Caitlin asked.

"Hard to tell. With Matt it took about a day. Though it might be different from person to person," I said.

"Come on, Caitlin, don't do this," Specs said.

"It's what I want."

Specs kicked a small trash can across the room and stormed out. I nodded to Baja to go keep an eye on him. Caitlin coughed a few times. Her face was pale, and she was beginning to sweat.

Benjamin walked over to the blacked-out window. It was covered in thick black paint. A small portion had been scratched away letting in a laser-tight beam of daylight. He leaned against the wall and stared out.

Without looking at us he spoke, "You can stay here the night. One of you will need to..."

"We know," Dax replied.

Over the following several hours we sat in moderate silence. There were few words exchanged, as it seemed no one knew what to say. We hadn't got to know Caitlin very well. What I knew of her were tidbits of information from our time in school together. But those days were long behind us. It wasn't just the fact that she wanted to die that made each of us feel low. It was the fact that we had gone to all the trouble to rescue her and her sister only to see them die. It was like a kick to the gut. If we couldn't save people, what was the point in trying? And yet something inside of us, a small quiet voice that tries to guide our lives, seemed to show us what was the right thing to do, even if we couldn't control the final outcome.

And that was the truth. None of us could ever

control what would happen today or tomorrow. We couldn't make someone want to live. It had to be their choice. What would we gain if we forced her to live only to watch her die later? If she wanted out, she would find it.

Suicide in an apocalypse was easy, and for some even more justified.

I could almost sense that we knew there had to be rules. Something to keep us from stepping over the line. In a world with no government or laws, it would be easy to make others do what we thought was right. But who was to say what was beneficial now?

That evening we ate pork and beans out of cans. We were right next to a whole foods store and eating processed food. The irony.

I cast a glance at Benjamin wondering what his story was. Any one of us could have overpowered him. Why did he help?

* * *

I would like to say it was a restful night of sleep but

it wasn't. Caitlin turned sometime in the early hours of the morning. Izzy had taken it upon herself to end it. Caitlin didn't want to shoot herself before she turned. It never ceased to amaze me how badly I felt after losing someone that I had only briefly known. Though it was the same long before the apocalypse. Every year I would hear of someone who had passed away from cancer, suicide, or an overdose. It would hit me in the core. I would feel the loss, regardless of how well I knew them. Maybe it's because we are all connected in some unseen way?

Benjamin had closed the rolling shutters later that evening. The use of blacked-out paint was to prevent anyone who might be passing by from seeing light. He covered the small area that wasn't painted with duct tape. In the morning he removed it and looked out. We didn't learn much from him that night. He was quiet and aloof. That morning he had made it known that when this had all kicked off he was part of the police department. He was one of the SWAT team. He didn't really own the stores, but he had made them his own. For the longest of time he lived off food from the shelves next door. It was eventually raided by a gang. Thankfully he had managed to keep them out of Wilderness Outfitters with the shutters. The fake wall he'd built was his final form of protection. It worked well because it was pitch-dark inside. Anyone else would have just seen a dead end at the end of a hallway.

"Have you seen many of these gangs?" I asked, lighting a cigarette.

He laughed. "This city is full of them."

"Where are they? We never saw them coming in."

"You will. They are out there, like rats. I'm sure they are holed inside an apartment or the shopping center."

"You make it sound as though there are a lot of them."

Benjamin pulled away from the window to look at me.

"Most days of the week my team and I were raiding

drug houses in the city. There are over three hundred gangs in this region. You think the Z's are deadly? You don't want to encounter them. They are merciless."

He returned to looking out.

"So why haven't you left here?" Dax asked, scooping melon from a can into his mouth.

"Where would I go?"

"I don't know. Look for others?"

He scoffed. "People are dead. This is it. This is life now."

"So you are just going to stay holed up in this place? What about when all the food is gone?"

"I'll go out for more and bring it back."

"Come with us. We could use a man of your skills."

He shook his head. "Where are you going?"

"Wherever they were broadcasting from. That's where we're heading."

OVERRUN

Benjamin wasn't keen on going with us. His reluctance to leave was odd. He stood a better chance of survival in a group. But somehow he didn't see it that way. I assumed he was used to working with a team. That he would have jumped at the chance. I figured there was something that he wasn't telling us.

Johnny and the others crowded round a table and stared at the map of the city. Benjamin knew the place like the back of his hand. He mentioned that the signal could have been broadcast from any one of the three thousand radio stations, but more than likely it came from the CDC. He took a red marker and circled its location, then mapped out several routes. The closest to us was a large radio station. Benjamin said they were known for providing the latest news for Salt Lake City.

"You know what you are attempting is a suicide mission," he said.

"Every time we step a foot outside, it's potential suicide," I replied.

"If Z's don't get you, one of the gangs will."

"More reason for you to come with us. We could use the help," Johnny said.

He shook his head. "No."

"Ok, well, what about weapons?" Baja asked.

"Take whatever you can find from the storage out back. Most of the goods in the store itself were looted by a gang who broke in a few days ago. Thankfully they never made it to the storage area. There's an axe down there, bowie knives, a pump-action shotgun, three boxes of shells. I'm sure you'll be able to find some ammo for the assault rifles and well… just go take a look."

Baja, Specs, and Ralphie strolled off to see what could be used.

While Benjamin continued to show Johnny a few of the routes, I went over to Izzy. She was going through her regular routine of checking the ammo in the two handguns we had.

"How many bullets?" I asked.

"Four."

"Let's hope there's more in storage."

She nodded.

"How you doing?"

I cleared my throat and took a seat beside her. It had been a long time since we had made time to talk to each other.

"I've been meaning to say—"

"Don't," she cut me off before I could finish. "The past is the past."

I shrugged. Clearly she wasn't interest in rehashing the past. "Right."

She had good reason to be angry. I got up and walked away thinking about what had led up to this. Before I had left for the military, things were good between us.

I know I should have told her sooner about

enlisting, but I didn't. She didn't find out until a week before boot camp. She had been going through a lot with her family and had almost become dependent on having me around. Though she won't admit that.

Telling her about the military was like dropping a bomb. She didn't handle it well. That's when the blame game started. I was responsible for everything that was going wrong in her life. Up until that point we had been together for four years. It had always been us. I knew she wouldn't have coped even if I had told her earlier — that's why I held back.

It didn't help that a rumor was circulating around that I had found someone else. That wasn't true but it was the final nail in the coffin. Besides a few offhand comments we hadn't spoken since. I figured that wouldn't change.

* * *

Baja burst into the room wearing a bandolier of bullets across his chest and waving two handguns.

"Ay, amigos."

He was pumping the air with two CZ P-09s when one of them went off. A few chunks of ceiling tile dropped.

"Shit," Baja said, with a face now covered in white dust.

"Where the hell did you get this guy from?" Benjamin asked.

"He's special," Dax replied.

"Yeah. I figured. You might want to confiscate the guns from him before he shoots himself."

Ralphie came back with his arms full of ammo boxes, and an axe strapped to his back. Specs crept around the corner with a crossbow.

"That's mine," Jess hollered. He tossed her the crossbow.

"I'll take the shotgun," I approached Specs who had strapped it to his back.

"Dude, I want this," Specs said, reluctant to give it up.

"Yeah, right."

Specs shook his head and handed it over. It was a Benelli SuperNova Tactical Pump-Action Shotgun. It was as slick as shit. I held it up and peered down the sight.

"How many does it hold?"

"Four, two and three-quarter shells," Specs rattled off the details as if he had been part of the manufacturing of the damn thing.

"Sweet."

"Any handguns?" Dax asked.

"Take your pick," Ralphie returned from another trip out back and slid a box full of various pieces across the floor. Dax took out a couple of Sig Sauers.

"Don't take them all. I'm gonna need some," Benjamin added.

"Right, but if you come with us..."

"Like I said. I go it alone."

"Your funeral, man," Baja replied.

"And knives?"

Specs tossed a Swiss Army knife to Dax and was about to show more when Baja stopped him with a hand on his arm. "Please. Allow me."

He crouched down over a box. He wrapped a piece of rag around his head. Seconds later he came up holding two huge bowie knives and spoke in a shit Australian accent.

"That ain't a knife, this is a knife."

"Okay, I don't know whether to shoot him or find the nearest mental hospital and drop him off," Dax replied shaking his head.

I came over and tapped him on the arm and took one of the knives.

"Nice touch with the bandana, man, but I think that's Rambo, dude, not Crocodile Dundee," I said.

"What can I say, I like to mix it up."

Once we were all geared up, one by one we thanked Benjamin. Somehow I sensed we would see him again. He told us to wait while he made sure the coast was clear. We were downstairs when we heard his foot tap twice indicating it was all good to go. I was the last one out. I pulled down the metal shutters and glanced up at the small hole. I gave a short nod and then we took off.

At least now we felt prepared for whatever came our way. We had eaten well, and with our bellies full and plenty of ammo, we made our way through the back streets of the city. Benjamin had marked out two routes just in case one of them didn't work out.

"So we'll make our way to the CDC and stop at that radio station on the way."

"What are you hoping to find, Dax?" Izzy asked. She obviously was unconvinced by his leadership skills.

"Maybe they left a note. I don't know."

"You don't know? I wish we had just stayed. I think Benjamin was right. We are risking our lives right now for what?" Izzy asked.

Dax spun around to Izzy. "You want to hole up inside there like him? That's no way to live. We need to find these safe zones."

"And what if there aren't any? Huh?"

Izzy just shook her head and pushed by him. Dax grabbed her by the arm.

"Get off, Dax, I mean it."

Dax stared at her.

"Dax," I said. Then as if snapping out of it, he let her go.

* * *

As we turned into an alley we came to a halt. The dead were all over the place. Halfway up there was a turn to the right. That was our exit. But there were at least twenty shuffling around in the alley.

"Lock and load," Dax said.

"Don't you mean load and lock?" Specs tried to correct Dax. It didn't go over well.

"Time to see if these shrimps slice up well," Baja took out two jagged-edged bowie knives.

"Dude, we aren't getting through them with knives," I said.

I raised my shotgun and one by one started unloading rounds into the Z's. They dropped like flies. Each of us moved forward, while Baja and Specs covered our backs. Ralphie was meant to keep an eye on the roofs above. We moved as one tight formation. We had no idea if and when gang members would show up. But if they were going to find us, it would be now. We were making plenty of noise. On top of all of that, we were attracting even more Z's.

"How we doing?" Specs yelled.

"Nearly there."

The plan was to pull in two of the dumpsters behind us as we got into the alley to decrease the amount of Z's that would get through. What we didn't bank on when making that right turn was coming face-to-face with another horde. The entire alley was packed. There was no way we were going to make it.

"We need to get the hell off the ground!" I yelled.

Unfortunately, there was no fire escape. The nearest one was further down.

"What do we do?" Specs asked.

"Specs, Baja, grab those dumpsters and move them forward," Jess yelled, taking charge.

All of the alleyways in the city had these large metal

dumpsters where all the trash was thrown out. Some of them were partially empty, but most were filled to the brim. Many of the black trash bags were stacked up against the sides. The whole alley stunk like the back end of a cow's dirty ass. Z's snarled and moaned like filthy animals. Several of the fast ones had managed to break through the group. One knocked Jess to the ground. I would have helped her but we were all trying to keep back the surge that felt like an ocean's tide pushing up against a shore. At this rate we were going to blow through all the ammo we had in a matter of minutes.

I turned to see Jess stabbing the grotesque beast in the eye. Blood spewed over her face. Thick globs ran down her cheeks as she shoved it off only to find herself wrestling with two more. I fired two rounds and they dropped, covering her like blankets.

"There's too many," Izzy yelled.

It didn't matter how many we killed, ten more took their place. The alley was filling up fast. The noise of their moans was horrendous.

"Get in."

I lifted the metal lid on the dumpster and Izzy and Ralphie jumped in. On the opposite side Dax had already climbed into one and was providing cover to Baja and Specs. One of the Z's had managed to grab a hold of Baja's pants and they were now halfway down his legs exposing his naked ass. My heartbeat felt like it was pumping a million times a minute. I didn't have a chance to see what happened to Jess. The lid slammed down and then it was like being inside a casket. Echoes of meaty hands and knees slamming up against the dumpster were only made worse by the sound of their snarling.

It had spiraled out of control real fast.

There must have been thousands turned in the city. While they weren't all together in one spot, there were enough of them to make Castle Rock's attack look like child's play.

Ralphie had his hands pressed over his ears. Izzy must have expected the lids to open any second as she had her assault rifle aimed up.

The clatter didn't ease up. I thought it would never end. How long we were inside was anyone's guess. Time ceased to exist. The smell entering my nostrils was beyond anything I had ever experienced. It wasn't just the aroma of trash. It was the smell of death.

All I could think about was Jess. Her body covered in three Z's, blood all over her as more Z's piled over the top clawing their way forward, eager to sink teeth into flesh.

As we waited for the living dead to move on we stared at each other in the darkness. Our eyes had adjusted. The only light came from the end of our guns. The glow lit up the inside and brought home the reality of what we were sitting on. It wasn't just bags. It was dead bodies. Izzy screamed when she saw a hand. Ralphie's cry wasn't much different. Instantly we thought the worst. Were they Z's, or humans about to turn?

Any second now I was expecting one of them to bite my nads. But in the whole time we'd been trapped in there, none of them moved. I swept light down on the face of one of them. A dark hole penetrating its forehead brought a wave of relief. Someone had killed them and tossed their bodies inside. Why? They weren't Z's? Had they been bitten? Had they attempted to clean up the streets? Perhaps they knew that the entire city was about to turn.

What had they experienced? I thought about what it must have been like to have been in a city full of Z's.

Ralphie laid his gun down and reached into the pocket of one of the dead. He pulled out a wallet and cracked it open.

"Fifty bucks, well how about that?"

He tossed it to one side, then retrieved the victim's ID.

"A Michael Wentworth. He was a medic." Izzy and I just listened in as he continued to rattle on about some stranger that none of us knew or even cared about. But someone did. Were they dead too?

As Ralphie continued rooting through the man's pockets, I moved up and cracked the lid ever so slightly. I wanted to get a better look at where Jess was. I could see the Z's but not her. She was gone.

"Psst! Hey," I tried my best to call to the others who were in the green metal dumpster across from us. A zombie turned and fixed its milky eyes on me and started shuffling over.

"Guys, is Jess in there?"

The lid went up a little. It was Dax. He just shook his head.

I didn't need to close the dumpster lid as a Z fell against it. I caught my finger between the lid and the rim. I shook my hand, grimacing in pain, and began to chuckle at my own stupidity.

"What are you laughing at?"

My head dropped. That's when I heard a knock. From below us, it occurred twice.

"You hear that?" Izzy asked.

It was muted by the layer of dead that we were sitting on but at the same time clearly it was a knock. I slid my hand down through the mess of rotting flesh and knocked twice. The knock happened again.

"It's Jess," I said.

"You sure?"

I straightened back up. "She must have crawled underneath the dumpster."

I lifted the lid. "That you, Jess?" I whispered.

"Yep."

"You okay?"

"No bites."

I lowered the lid again, relieved that she was still alive, and unharmed. We must have been inside that dumpster for the better part of three hours. That's how long it took before the Z's moved out. By the time Jess felt safe enough to slide out and join us, there were only ten remaining Z's by my estimate. The others had wandered off into the city. Over the course of those three hours we heard gunfire a few times. There were others out there. Were they the gangs that Benjamin spoke of? We had no way of knowing. Maybe they were like us? Those who were seeking other survivors. Trying to stay alive and keep their sanity in the process.

102.5 THE WOLF

It was late afternoon when we rolled out. We stunk to high heaven but we were alive. Jess told us that if it hadn't been for the three dead Z's that had covered and smothered her like a blanket she wouldn't have survived. Over the course of an hour she shuffled on her back using the dead Z's as a shield until she had reached the dumpster. She then hid beneath it.

"You look like you are a newborn baby," Izzy remarked as we tried to wipe off the grime. We had got used to smelling bad. It was odd how much hygiene was taken seriously before all this. Now, we didn't care. Survival was more important.

While the CDC was where we ultimately wanted to go, we had initially targeted 102.5 The Wolf, a radio station. It was the largest of all the broadcasting stations in the city. Based on Benjamin's advice, he felt that the signal could have only come from one of those two places. Knowing our luck, it never came from any of them. Izzy had argued home the point that anyone could have broadcast it. The city was overrun with the dead. The chances of finding where that initial broadcast came from was like searching for a needle in a haystack.

There were only five Z's left in the alley, Baja finished them off with the axe Izzy was carrying. He looked like Thor wielding it, whereas she looked like she was trying to retrieve the sword in the stone. She could barely lift it, and she was a fit girl. How the hell she had managed to strap it to her back was beyond me. Both of them had got into a bit of a pissing match over who should have it. Eventually, Jess told her to let it go.

Baja was a bit of an oddball that way. Most of the time he was pretty lighthearted, but he could be pushy at times and a bit of an asshole when he wanted to be. Then again all of us could.

As much as the others were complaining about

having to haul ass over to the radio station, I understood why Dax wanted to go. Even if the signal hadn't come out of there, there was a possibility the equipment might be working off a generator. If it was, we might have been able to contact someone. It was a long shot. We knew that.

I had noticed that Dax and Izzy were once again keeping their distance. I shook my head in complete amazement. If ever there was a time to bury the hatchet, it was now. None of us knew if we were going to make it through the day. Petty disagreements seemed pointless.

We were in this together. Family. The only ones who would watch out for each other. In the short time together I had noticed how quick each of us listened to the other, even if we did moan over decisions made.

Dax had given us this spiel about what they taught them in the military. That no matter what, when they were out in the field, they were to make sure that no one was left behind. Of course there would be times when the enemy would overtake, when things would spiral out of control, but they were trained to look out for the safety of each other.

The station was three blocks from the alley. We stayed low, passing burnt-out cars. The charred remains of bodies lined the streets. Those who must have been attacked by gangs were brutalized. Their bodies strung up on fences or posts, or nailed to walls. Graffiti had been sprayed all over them. They showed no mercy.

We managed to get to the other side of the block with minimal interference from Z's. A couple of times we had to hold our position under trucks until a group of walkers passed by. It wasn't that we couldn't have taken them out. But our best defense was not attacking it was avoidance. Anything else was a last resort, a means to an end to get us through dangerous sections of the city.

As we drew closer to the radio station located across from a large city park, we noticed there were heads everywhere. Someone had decapitated and strung them up like Christmas decorations. Their faces were battered as if someone had taken a pickaxe to them.

There was no point in telling Jess or Izzy not to look. They were as accustomed to the horrors of the apocalypse as much as us. You didn't grimace at every sight. You became numb to it. The shock it once held was now gone.

102.5 The Wolf radio operated out of a large glass building. It must have been in pristine condition at one time. Now the bottom quarter of it was caved in from a truck that had careened into the side. Concrete steps and a part of an elevator were exposed. Its metal doors were crushed and bent. Rubble, papers, and blood were everywhere. The stench that hit us as we moved in was like a wall. Electrical wires that were no longer live hung down like spider legs.

We moved with our backs to the wall at a fair clip trying to get inside before the batch of Z's that were shuffling around across the road spotted us.

"Wait." Dax held up a clenched fist. We dropped behind a burnt-out cab. At first I thought he had spotted a horde of Z's. But that wasn't it. The sound of wheels slowly churning over filled the air. It got louder, until we saw a forest-green tank come around the corner. We figured it was military doing their rounds searching for survivors. It wasn't. Five men dressed in blue bandanas controlled it. One of them was driving; another was manning the machine gun on the front and taking potshots at Z's. The other three were spread out over the front and back with assault rifles. One of them threw a grenade. Another fired a rocket launcher at thirty Z's in the distance. The echo shook the ground. A cloud of smoke and debris went into the air. That was followed by laughter. They loved every minute.

"Stay low," Dax whispered.

We hugged the ground. The only things between us and them were two vehicles.

"Homie, get the three on the left," we heard one of them shout out.

"Ah, look at that bitch's tits hanging out. Watch this."

I peered around the cab in time to see some female

Z get her body drilled and rearranged by an excessive amount of bullets. They didn't aim for the head. It fell to the floor.

"I'm grabbing it as a mascot," one of them barked.

Two of them jumped down, grabbed her arms, and began dragging this thing across the ground while the others covered them. They tore off what remaining clothes were clinging to her body and then impaled her on the tank's gun like a soft toy on the front of a Mack truck. The large, lengthy barrel went through her chest like a knife slices warm butter. The Z's legs dangled there while it gnashed its teeth. If that wasn't bad enough, the two men sat on the front of the tank laughing, and taking turns spanking her rotten, mutated ass.

This was nothing but a game to them. The tank surged forward rolling over Z's that attempted to reach them. Blood splattered. Jess shook her head.

"Animals."

We waited until they were gone before we slipped inside the radio station. The stairs had been partially blown out. We had to jump three steps just to continue. Within a matter of minutes, we were on the second floor. We stared at the offices in complete disarray, wondering what they must have gone through when this had hit the city. Had it been night or day when the infected struck? Did they have time to escape?

"Stay tight," Dax said as he took the lead. We were looking for the main studio. We passed by several framed pictures on the walls of guests that had attended the station. There were the Rolling Stones, Rod Stewart, the Dixie Chicks, and a whole host of bands that had made a name for themselves. There was more than one control room that would have been used for live radio. We peered in thinking that no one was there. I saw a large desk with computers and microphones all over the floor. A smeared blood handprint on a window separated the hall and room. As I got closer a Z came into view. At first it startled me. I jumped back. It smashed repeatedly on the thick glass. Each time a part of its face would cave in.

We soon came to realize this wasn't just one radio

station but seven combined into one facility. We split up. Dax went with Izzy, Jess came with me, and the other three went up to the next floor.

"How are you coping?" I asked Jess. The whole incident back in the alley had shaken her up. We'd come close to losing her. We all realized that it could happen to any one of us. That's why we had already said our goodbyes. I know, it sounds odd, but we had to be realistic. The idea that we were going to live long into our sixties, see grandkids, and wind up in a nursing home was a joke now. There was more chance of us getting bit before the day was out. We'd told each other that if things did go bad, no one would get to decide how we would end it. Whether that meant turning the gun on ourselves or waiting until we turned, we each got to choose how we would go.

And yet, all of us had said we would rather shoot ourselves than turn.

"I'm as well as I can be under the circumstances," she replied.

"Over there."

We stood at a corner. Inside a control room three Z's walked back and forth. One of them had its arm ripped off, another, part of its jaw hung low. The sound of my blade coming out of the sheath was all it took for Jess to know what to do. She moved close to the door, gave me a nod, twisted the handle, and I booted it open. We had learned it was best to let them come to us when faced with a room. Only a few could get through the door at one time. In this case the door was only wide enough for one. I stabbed, retracted the blade. It dropped. Jess followed suit with the next and I finished off the last.

On the wall inside smeared in blood were the words, *Long Live The President!*

"Odd thing to write. If I was about to die, I would be more inclined to write the words, fuck this life, or suck my dick, Z's. But instead someone writes, LONG LIVE THE PRESIDENT?"

"Maybe they were patriotic."

"Patriotism I'm pretty sure came to an end when

this great nation did."

We began looking around inside the booth for anything. Notes, anything that might have been left behind. Some indication that whoever was here knew about a safe zone.

"You think there are people still in the White House?"

"If they are, they're probably dead."

"But I mean, continuity of government and such? They are usually prepared for the worst-case scenario. You know, mass evacuation and relocation of federal government agencies and the White House," Jess added.

I heard her but wasn't paying attention. I had put on a pair of blood-stained headphones and was playing with dials. There was nothing. If they had a generator it wasn't on.

"Let's keep moving."

* * *

On the next level Baja, Specs, and Ralphie were exploring the rooms.

"I'm thinking I could have been a radio presenter," Baja muttered as they peered around corners fully expecting a hungry Z to pop out.

"Really? Give me your best radio voice," Specs replied.

Baja tucked his handgun away, cupped his hands over his mouth, and cleared his throat.

"Puh, puh, one, two, one two. This one goes out to all the brothers and bitches."

Specs immediately cut him off. "Okay, you're meant to be doing a radio broadcast not preparing for a rap battle."

"I know, I know. Hold up. I was just getting warmed up."

Ralphie smirked as he covered them from behind.

Baja took a deep breath and then belted out, "Good morning, Vietnam."

Specs and Ralphie cracked up.

"Dude, that was Robin Williams."

"I know. He was the king radio."

"He was an actor playing a radio presenter."

"Whatever."

"Let me have a try," Ralphie said, straightening up. He stood in front of the other two and took a deep breath.

"Zombies," he muttered in a barely audible voice

"Oh man, that was shit. Even worse than mine," Baja said.

"I dunno about that, yours was pretty bad," Specs retorted.

"Z-Z-Zombies."

"Okay, what is that meant to be? Reverb?"

Ralphie's eyes went as wide as two large coins. Specs cast a glance over his shoulder.

"Oh shit."

Coming down behind them were seven Z's. All of them were obese, probably the result of spending all their time sitting down doing radio shows and eating nothing but vending machine food. One of them looked like he must have been a body builder in his past life. The guy had more meat on him than a pregnant cow, even after he'd died.

Baja twisted around, thinking they were winding him up. By that point they were just a few feet away. He reached for his two guns and fired round after round. The entire hall filled with dust as they unloaded their weapons. Specs jumped back just in time as the first Z came down hard on Baja. Another followed. One by one they collapsed on top of each other. Then it went quiet. Somewhere at the bottom below it all was Baja gasping for air.

"Get these fat fuckers off me."

Specs and Ralphie chuckled.

"Now that wasn't a bad radio voice," Specs said, between laughing.

"Yeah, that was actually pretty damn good."

"Glad you liked it. Now, a little help!"

* * *

Down below Dax and Izzy were scouting around. They were having about as much luck as the rest of them.

There was nothing but empty rooms and the odd Z kicking around.

“So what do you miss?” Izzy tried to make small talk with Dax.

Dax was easing a door open with the tip of his barrel. “What?” he replied, barely hearing her.

“You know, since all this shit happened. What do you miss?”

He smirked. “Big Macs and fries.”

“Come on,” she groaned.

“Truthfully?” he asked.

“Yeah.”

He paused, doing one final check in another control room.

“Sex.”

She huffed. “Oh you would. You always were a horn dog.”

He let out a chuckle, keeping his eyes fixed ahead of him. The lighting in half the hallway was out and there was very little daylight making its way in. Darkness covered the tail end of the hall.

"I think we'll leave that part. Let's head back."

"What about in here?"

Izzy ducked into a room without any thought to what might be hiding in the shadows. Up until that point they had been so careful.

"Izzy," Dax called out when he turned and saw she wasn't there.

A second later she poked her head around the corner.

"Nah, nothing in there. Though, there was this."

She held out a half-empty bottle of Jack Daniel's.

"Oh, you beauty," he replied.

She twisted off the top and took a swig before handing it to Dax who gulped it down like water.

Izzy sat back on the table. Dax handed the bottle back. He felt her hand touch his and she lingered there for a second.

"Izzy, it wasn't all bad, was it?"

She locked eyes with him.

"No, I guess not."

"You know my father was pressuring me to go into the Marines."

She dropped her eyes. "Yeah, I realize that."

He stepped in closer to her.

"For what it's worth, I'm sorry. That rumor about me and that other girl." He shook his head. "Never happened."

She looked up and then rose to her feet as if realizing that he was closing the gap. They studied each other's face. Dax moved nearer, feeling the chemistry they had once had, if only for a moment. He was about to kiss her when he heard Johnny.

"Dax, Izzy, let's go!"

"I guess we should go," Izzy said before slipping past him.

Dax squeezed his eyes shut and blew out his cheeks. He was so close.

THUG LIFE

We hadn't made it even a mile when the dead spotted us again. At first there were about five milling around a dumpster. The smell that lingered in the air was even more putrid. Each of us masked up our faces with bandanas just to prevent ourselves from becoming sick.

"Save your bullets."

I pulled out a machete, Dax had a knife. We prepared ourselves for a fight but decided to run for it. We dashed down a different street. One by one we checked the stores to find any that were open. It might have been possible, if we'd had more time. Problem was, some of the fast suckers were moving at breakneck speed towards us.

Before we could react, three flashbang canisters hit the floor. We had no clue who threw them, only that the explosion was deafening. As each of us dropped to the ground and began eying the windows above us, we didn't notice the surge of dead closing in on us. It had attracted them like moths to a flame.

Baja was the first to see it.

"Holy shit." Baja paused, his eyes widening. "Guys."

We turned to see the street behind us filling up with crawlers. It was beginning to look like a marathon run. From one side of the street to the next, lines of Z's stumbled forward moaning and gnashing their teeth. I thought we had seen a lot back in Castle Rock but that was nothing compared to this. The dead moved forward like an army from hell.

Specs was the first one to fire a round at one that burst out of a store. We followed suit turning on the balls of our feet and dashing toward another alley. We didn't select it because it looked empty. There was no other direction we could head in. Like rats coming out of the sewers, skin-eaters made their way towards us from every possible direction. Even in the alley, there were walkers. We hacked at their heads like a combine fucking harvester. Blood splattered against stone as we rushed forward.

Either side of the thin alley were industrial dumpsters. Jess and Izzy wanted to hide in them but with the mass of freaks coming for us it was possible that we would never get out. Instead we opted to jump up on a dumpster and climb over a tall fence that took us into another section of the alley. Baja spotted a fire escape about eight yards away. Its decaying black metal frame snaked up the side of a red brick building. Whether it could hold the weight of us all was doubtful, but right now all that mattered was avoiding becoming a human Happy Meal.

The noise and howls of the dead filled my mind with dread. Ralphie stumbled and the fence tore into his leg.

"Johnny," Jess called out.

I spun around and could see Jess trying to help

Ralphie.

"I got this," Baja said. He rushed back and took a hold of his hands and pulled him over. Meanwhile Dax and Specs fired at the Z's ahead of us. They were the only ones that were an immediate threat. The crowd of flesh-eaters that had initially come after us were pressing against the fence. There were so many, the ones at the front were pushed through the small openings in the metal fence like a fucked-up sausage grinder. I swear I nearly tossed up what little I had in my stomach at the sight.

One by one we ascended the metal staircase. It creaked and groaned its age. The fire escape wasn't firmly fixed against the side of the stone, so there was a chance that we could end up shaking it loose and dropping to our deaths.

"I'm okay, I can do it myself," Izzy said as Baja was trying to yank her up by the scruff of her collar.

When we reached the top, my hands were shaking. I looked down at the mass of distorted pale faces chomping the air. Their milky eyes fixed on ours. Their fingers tore at the brick, unable to climb. Ralphie toppled over onto the roof, clasping his leg trying to stop the bleeding. Izzy didn't hesitate; she tore off some of her pant leg and wrapped it around his wound.

"Fuck this place. What the hell is there here for us? They are all dead," Specs barked.

"Calm down," I replied.

"I should have just died back in Castle Rock with my family."

I took a hold of him and gave a shake. "Snap out of it."

It was hard to take it all in. The noise of the dead below, Ralphie in tears, and Specs pacing back and forth looking as if he was about to leap off.

"Listen, whoever threw those canisters are alive. There are others here. We just need to find them."

"Oh, you think they were trying to help us. Please. They made it worse," Specs said.

"Maybe, but maybe not. All I know is we need food and perhaps they have some."

"I highly doubt they're going to invite us to an all-you-can-eat buffet. They just tried to make us one for those fuckers down there."

"You need to settle down," Dax said to Specs. Specs shook his head and wandered over to the opposite edge to gaze down at the street below.

"You okay, Jess?" I asked. Her hands were shaking. I took a hold of them and stared into her eyes, trying to gauge if she was still with us. The truth was, it would have been very easy for all of us to lose it. All sense of normality was gone. Nothing remained except a world that was trying to kill. Every waking moment was filled with a sense of dread. Who would be next to go? What would happen if we fell into the wrong hands? If we didn't get any food soon, would we starve to death?

"What now?" I asked Dax.

"Stop asking that," he shot back.

"I was just—"

"I don't know, Johnny. This is as foreign to me as you."

There it was. I had finally seen a crack in Dax's hard exterior. I could see the look on his face. Perplexed, overwhelmed, and confused. Naturally, because he was the oldest among us and my brother, I looked to him for answers. But there were none.

We were living hour to hour hoping to stay alive and we had no way of knowing if we would. We had barely caught our breath when we heard a stranger's voice.

"Toss your weapons down."

I spun around with my shotgun pointed at two masked individuals. They wore black bandanas over the bottom part of their faces. Both had white skulls on them. From the little I could see, they both looked African American.

"We will end you right here. Now put them down."

"I think you are little outnumbered," Dax said scowling at them.

"Really?"

The man pulled his banana down to reveal a smirk

and goatee. His eyes looked around. We followed his gaze to see even more guns pointed at us from adjoining buildings above and to the left and right. There had to have been fifteen of them. Each of them wore the same skull bandana.

We cast a nervous glance at each other before reluctantly placing our assault rifles, shotgun, and other weapons on the floor. One of the two approached with a large duffel bag and scooped them up.

"Pleasure doing business with you."

They turned to leave.

I stepped forward "What, that's it? You are going to leave us without nothing to defend ourselves with?"

The man with the goatee turned back. He paused before reaching into the bag. He removed a Beretta. Took out the magazine, tossed the handgun near my feet, and threw the magazine over the edge. Right below to where the crowd of Z's were.

"Happy?"

"You fucking piece of shit," I said.

My nostrils flared and I heard the click of guns as I moved forward on him. It was mad really. We didn't know them from jack, and had no way of knowing if they would kill us. But then again we had already encountered our fair share of lunatics. I wasn't thinking clearly.

"Be grateful we aren't tossing you over the edge."

"Why?" Jess asked. "Why are you doing this?"

The one who had taken down his bandana was about to answer when the other pulled him away. The guy with the goatee jerked his arm away.

He snorted and turned back to Jess. "You aren't from around here, are you?"

She shook her head. "Where we come from we wouldn't rob people of their weapons."

Baja tossed her a look and for a moment you could have heard crickets. We had attempted to do exactly that back at the silo. Though, the difference was they were ours to begin with, and those guys were royal dicks. They had what was coming to them.

He studied all of us with a look of amusement.

Before any more words were exchanged, gunfire erupted and all of us scrambled for cover. At first I thought they had decided to kill us. But that wasn't it. I looked up to see them returning fire across the street to another building. There were even more figures on the other side than the ones we had encountered. I couldn't tell who they were. All of us were crawling on our hands and knees trying to get behind the numerous metal air vents.

"Reapers," one of them yelled.

"How the hell do we find all the idiots?" Baja yelled from behind cover.

"Maybe you're a douche magnet," Izzy shot back.

I called out to the man with the goatee. "You want to toss me a gun?" He just smirked and continued firing. They all looked like this was just another day in the hood.

"What the hell is going on?" Ralphie bellowed.

Bullets were pinging off steel and ricocheting. You could hear the snap of them whizzing past us. We saw one of their men fall off the adjoining building onto the roof.

His body hit with a thud. Blood pooled from his head.

Dax gestured to me. The two men with the bag were busy returning fire, paying no attention to our weapons. I was the closest. Though to reach it I would have to expose myself to the roof across from us. The same one where gang members were snapping up shit like it was a Mexican fiesta.

I took a deep breath and rolled across. A bullet tore up the concrete in front of me, inches from my hand. I leapt for the bag and managed to get one out when one of the skulled men turned and kicked me back. He didn't have time to fight. All he could do was grab the bag and dash into the stairwell. I chased after him, returning fire. A round hit him in the shoulder and he fell backwards down the first flight of stairs.

"The next one is going in your head."

I felt a gun press against the back of my head.

"Now drop it."

Gunfire was still erupting outside. I let the CZ P-09 fall from my hand to the floor.

"Joshua, you okay?"

"I've been hit, Elijah."

"If he dies, you die. Now go." He pushed me forward toward the stairs. I turned to see him whistle to the others. They jumped down from the adjoining buildings and muscled the others in our group into the stairwell. It didn't take us long to reach the ground floor. We found ourselves inside a grocery store. No doubt there was no food. The place smelled bad as though someone had unplugged all the fridges and meat had turned rotten. That was exactly it. There was no power, and everything had been left to decay.

We waited for what seemed like another ten minutes as the rest of their surviving men returned with a vehicle. It was a cube van. They piled us inside and then zip-tied each of us.

"Go," Elijah yelled.

"Who are you?" I asked.

"We go by the name BMGs or TBKs"

"Is that like MSGs?" Baja asked

"Yeah, keep it up. And you'll be the first one to go."

One of the other masked men spoke up. "The Black Mafia, or otherwise known as the Dark Kings, heard of us?"

"I'd like to say I have, but no. But I have heard of your rival gang. The TTs."

"Who?" he replied.

"The Teletubbies," I replied.

Baja smirked. Elijah just gave me a cold stare.

"Where are you taking us?" Dax asked.

"You'll see."

THE DARK KINGS

We were hustled towards a cinema. The front doors had been boarded up with planks of wood and sheets of steel. A few bangs on the front entrance and someone peeked out. Once all of us were in, we noticed there were a lot of them just milling around. They stared at us inquisitively.

We were led into a back office. The door slammed behind us.

"Hey," Izzy yelled kicking the door.

"Settle down, sweet cheeks," Baja said.

"What did you call me?"

Izzy shook her head then continued to kick the door.

"Well this is grand," Specs said.

"Yeah."

I slumped down against the wall. They had stripped out everything from inside the office. There were no windows. All that remained was a clock on the wall that no longer worked. It wouldn't have mattered. Time ceased to exist in this new world. There were no schedules, places to be. It was actually refreshing. No more trying to keep up with a fast-paced society, or reading quotes about how life was short so use every minute. The apocalypse had brought a whole new meaning to life expectancy.

After a while, the door opened and Elijah came back in. Behind him were two men with plastic plates of food, and bottles of water. Up until that point we could hear a lot of talk outside. It was muffled but heated.

"Eat up."

"How's your friend?" I asked.

"You're lucky. He'll survive."

As he turned to leave I got up.

"How long are you going to keep us here?" I asked.

"Until we make sure there aren't any more of you."

"Well that's easy to clear up. There isn't."

"That's what they all say."

"All?"

"Gangs."

Baja snorted. "You think we're a gang?"

"Well, aren't you?"

"Oh, you got us red-handed, I'm Al Capone," Baja muttered.

"Is that who was shooting at us?" I asked.

Elijah's eyes drifted from Baja to me. "Grim Reapers."

"Who the hell are they?"

He never answered. Instead he studied us before asking his own questions. "Where are you guys from?"

"Castle Rock," Jess said.

"What brought you here?"

"Our town was overrun. We heard a radio signal broadcasting from Salt Lake City. We thought there might be safe zones."

He laughed. "Safe zones? Nowhere is safe."

The other man with him tapped him but Elijah seemed interested in talking.

"Have you heard the broadcast?" Dax asked.

He nodded exhaling cigarette smoke.

"Where's it coming from?"

"It's broadcast out of the CDC."

"There's other survivors?"

He looked at us as if we were from another planet. "There was."

Each of us started eating the food we were given. It was sliced Spam.

"Why do they keep broadcasting?" I asked.

Elijah looked at the other guys with him.

"Probably best I show you."

We all rose to our feet.

He shook his head. "No, just you." He pointed to me.

The others looked at me, concerned. "I'll be all right."

I couldn't say for sure if I would or not. Call it a

hunch or gut instinct but something told me Elijah was different from the others. As we left the room I walked in step with Elijah who gestured to two others to come with us.

"Why didn't you shoot me?" I asked

"What?"

"Back on the roof. After I shot your friend."

"Maybe I will."

We moved fast between buildings. I got a sense that it wasn't because of Z's but the threat of an attack from another gang. Eventually we arrived inside a tall office block. It was mostly made from glass. We ascended stairs two at time until we were on the sixteenth floor. There, Elijah led me to a window that overlooked the city.

I looked out over the vast desolate city. A huge building rose up in the distance.

"What is that?"

"Temple Square. It's run by the Grim Reapers. A motherfucker by the name of Domino is in charge. After the city was taken over by the dead, they took up residence there."

Temple Square was a ten-acre complex at the heart of Salt Lake City. An entire block surrounded by a fifteen-foot wall. Though it looked as if the Reapers had created their own wall from sheets of corrugated metal to fill in the gaps. The surrounding city was built around it when the Mormons established themselves back in 1847. Inside, at the center was a magnificent granite structure. It was built like a fortress. Its spires rose up among the downtown buildings, shopping malls, and beautiful landscapes. It reminded me of Disney Castle.

"And the CDC?"

"West. Further down. About an eleven-minute drive."

I nodded. "Why are you showing me this?"

He looked at me. "Because you guys look green." He chuckled to himself. "There is a war taking place that's far more dangerous than those walkers you see out there. You are more liable to die from a stray bullet than being bitten. The Reapers run everything."

"And police?"

He let out a chuckle. "You've got to be kidding. Those pussies bolted or were killed the moment everything went to hell."

"And what about your group?"

"There are over two hundred Reapers, and sixty of us. They keep to their side, we keep to ours."

"If there are no safe zones, why don't you leave?"

"This is our home."

"That's what I said about Castle Rock. Things are different now."

"Maybe for you, but not for us. Come. We should go, you don't want to be out here after dark."

As we made our way back, I noticed how few people we saw on the streets. It seemed the only ones that had survived were the gangs. Those willing to kill, those who had spent their entire lives preparing for the worst-case scenario. Though for them, it was prison time or a gangland hit.

We were three blocks from their base when one of

his men was shot. The bullet came out of nowhere. It echoed. We scrambled for cover. Elijah had his eyes on the rooftops. I stared at his friend who was still alive but not moving.

"Darius, go get Lukas," Elijah yelled.

"Fuck that homie!" Darius said before returning fire and then making a run for it. Darius was the only one that was close to a door that led into a building. Every time we tried to see if the coast was clear, bullets would snap past our heads. They had us pinned down in an alley behind a couple of industrial dumpsters. Several gunshots were coming from either side. Maybe I was mad or angry at being held against our will but I just wanted to get the hell out of there. At the same time I knew what it was like to lose someone. To be pushed into a corner and fired upon. I dived out into the open area, grabbed a hold of Lukas, and dragged him to the other side of the alley.

Lukas had been hit in the back. The chances of him surviving were slim. I took out his weapon that he had stashed in the back of his pants and began firing up at a

Hispanic guy that was taking shots from the roof. For those brief few minutes I had never felt my pulse race so hard. The noise of gunfire was attracting Z's. They had started to shuffle into the alley.

"Elijah, you are going to have to get over. We need to get out. I can't carry him by myself."

Elijah gave a nod.

"I'll cover you. On three."

I raised my fingers, counting up. On three he rolled, firing in the opposite direction while I continued laying heat on the guy above us. As soon as he was over he swung Lukas's arm around his shoulder.

"All right, buddy, we'll have you out of here."

"Go."

The door was a few feet from us. There was a good chance we would be hit with a bullet. But it was get out or end up some Z's Big Mac. Gasping for air as we made it into the building we didn't stop to check if anyone was following. We pressed on. Lukas was groaning.

"Stay with us," Elijah shouted.

Several Z's came in the door and were following. They were the slow suckers but liable to do some serious damage if they got hold of us.

"Go. I'll follow behind you," I said.

"I'm not leaving you," Elijah replied.

"Earlier you were going to shoot me. I think I'll be fine."

Elijah shook his head.

"Go," I repeated.

"You know your way back?"

I nodded.

Elijah stumbled forward dragging Lukas. I unloaded three rounds at the heads of two walkers who were spewing blood from their mouths.

"Damn, you are some ugly motherfuckers." Once they were down I kept inching back until I was at the door on the other side of the building. I slammed it closed and pushed a dumpster in front of it. The door jerked back and forth as I saw Z's trying to get out. I knew I wasn't going to be able to get through the next door as the alley was already filling up with more Z's. I clambered onto the dumpster and reached for the fire escape. It was out of reach. I pushed the gun into the small of my back and tried to steady my balance.

It was hard because the walkers were determined they were going to get through the metal door. The sound of metal pieces slapping up against each other and the sight of more shufflers coming into the alley got my ass in gear. I stepped back to the edge of the dumpster, took a few fast steps, and jumped off. I barely caught the bottom rung. I felt my elbow almost pop out of its socket as I hung by my fingers.

Beneath, reaching up at my feet were ten Z's. I could feel the tips of their fingers clawing at the soles of my boots. My fingers were slipping. It wasn't that I couldn't have pulled myself up if given time but they now had their chicken-licking fingers around the tips of my boot and probably were placing bets on who would get the first bite.

I felt like a stretchy toy being yanked back and

forth.

Suddenly gunfire. Thankfully this time it wasn't from the Grim Reapers. It was Elijah. He was standing just beyond a window across from me. He fired at the heads of Z's directly below. They flopped to the floor. I managed to grasp the next rung on the ladder and pull myself up. It took everything I had but once my feet touched the metal, I breathed a sigh of relief.

I quickly made my way up the ladder. At the edge I peeked over to make sure no Grim Reapers were on the roof before clambering over. I took a minute to catch my breath before assessing how the hell I was going to get out of there. As I hauled myself up. I looked across the rooftops. It was much higher up than those found in Castle Rock. For a second I found myself thinking of the old town. I felt a twinge of sadness.

It was quickly replaced by panic when a bullet zipped past. I turned my head to see one of the Reapers. They were dressed in black with a blue bandana. I returned fire, then bolted. In the distance I saw a thick pipe that extended across from one side of the building to the other. It had to have been part of the water or air ventilation system. I raced over to it, fired a few more rounds before doing a crazy balancing act. Below, the ground had to have been forty feet down. Z's shuffled around moaning and gazing up. Across the street on the opposite rooftop was a Reaper taking shots at me like a tin can. Yeah, you could say I wasn't having a good day.

As soon as I made it across I dashed to the emergency exit and entered the stairwell. My heart was beating a mile a minute.

I retraced my steps back to the cinema.

Elijah must have already made it back, as I didn't see him along the way. I had called out his name when I reached the ground but heard nothing except the moans of the dead.

* * *

From the moment I entered, I knew something was going down. The noise inside had reached an epic level. An argument had broken out between Darius and Elijah.

They were shoving each other back and forth.

"You abandoned us back there," Elijah barked.

"What did you expect me to do, homie?"

Elijah caught sight of me. I was sweating from running. He pointed at me.

"He's not even one of us. But he didn't run. Lukas would have been dead if it wasn't for him."

"Bullshit. If it wasn't for him, we wouldn't even be out there. I say we shoot that muthafuker." Darius pulled a Glock and before he had made it a few steps in my direction, Elijah had his own gun pressed against his temple.

"Put the gun down."

"Homie, what the fuck?"

"You're not my homie. You're a coward. You ran and left us behind. Now put it down. I won't say it again."

By now several of the other members had their guns drawn.

"I'm with Darius, I say we get rid of them."

"Fuck that. We do what Elijah says."

Some of them were pointing guns at Elijah, others were pointing them at those who were aiming at him.

There was some serious discord going on here.

"Settle down," I said, trying to catch my breath. Sweat was running down the side of my cheek. I had my hands on my knees. I was wiped out and in no mood for an argument. "We're alive, that's all that matters."

There was an awkward pause as each of them slowly backed off.

Elijah cast a glance at me and then looked at the others before shaking his head.

"Someone deal with Lukas. Get him patched up."

"Look, I'm sorry, man," Darius said.

"Get out of my sight," Elijah said before he came over to check on me. "You okay?"

"Yeah."

He placed a hand on my back.

"What you did back there. Why?"

I paused before answering. "I didn't do anything

anyone else wouldn't have done."

"Obviously you did."

He studied my face, nodding slowly. Elijah turned to another member of the Dark Kings.

"Let the others out."

He nodded and disappeared out back. Within a matter of a few minutes, Dax, Baja, and the others were released. They were rubbing their wrists after their binds had been cut.

"Tonight you join us to eat. Tomorrow, I'll get your guns, a few more supplies, and if you need to get out of the city, I'll show you how."

I nodded.

"What's your name?"

"Johnny. Johnny Goode."

He grasped my hand. "Thanks, man."

With that said, Elijah walked away. The others came over and started questioning me about what happened. I brought them up to speed. A few hours later they invited us into the main auditorium. Many of them looked at us and talked among themselves. While most were still standoffish, a couple came over and thanked me for helping. Lukas was lucky to have survived. Had the bullet been a few inches over, he would have been dead.

We each were given a paper plate of cooked chicken and a beer. We hadn't had anything like that in a long time. We had been living off MREs and vending machine crap for the past week. That evening we sat in the warmth of the cinema, feeling safe. We hadn't felt that way since arriving. Nothing had changed outside. The dead still wandered around looking for the next feast. Grim Reapers no doubt would be searching for those that had killed their own. But for now, we were alive.

COLOSSEUM

I woke up feeling better than I did the day before. We still stunk to high heaven but we were all able to get a good night's sleep. I rolled off the tiny bed the Dark Kings had stolen from a downtown shelter. Others slept on torn-up couches. It was the small things now that mattered most. Not feeling hunger, being able to sleep without fear of having your throat torn out.

My head ached a little and I needed coffee. I would have settled for the dregs at the bottom of a dumpster. Anything with caffeine. Dax and the others were already up and talking with Elijah. Rap music was playing quietly in the background.

"About time you woke up. I thought you were going to sleep all day," Jess said.

I stumbled over to them across an obstacle course of

shit that belonged to the gang. They had collected anything and everything that could be of use to them. Old portable radios, tools from hardware stores, furniture, a generator that looked as if it was still being worked on, but mostly canned food. That stuff was gold now.

"Where's the can?" I asked.

Elijah thumbed behind him. I strolled off.

As I was washing my hands in the washroom I noticed how scruffy my face had become. I hadn't shaved since the day before leaving Castle Rock. I ran a hand across my cheek. I was beginning to look like the wild man of Borneo.

A few minutes later Elijah came in. I nodded and we had this awkward moment that could only be encountered in a men's washroom. What was the deal with that? I mean, we all had the same faculties down below. But when you tossed in a few stalls, urinals, and sinks it brought a whole strange vibe to it all. Unless of course you were as drunk as a skunk, in which case you spent less time feeling self-conscious and more trying to piss straight.

I felt like saying, "So how about those Dodgers?" but I knew he would have replied, "They are dead."

Somehow it just wouldn't have had the same ring to it.

I was still trying to figure out if Elijah was the head honcho. The night before we never really came to know if the TBKs had a leader. Some had said the original one had died, others gestured to Elijah, while a few more said there was still a bit of a pissing match going on as to who should take charge.

While it seemed to matter to them, it didn't to Elijah. He'd told us of how he'd grown up around the TBKs. His eldest brother was a member long before he was, that was until he was murdered by the Grim Reapers. The only commonality between the TBKs and the Grim Reapers was they were all Mormons. In fact, it was uncommon if you weren't. But that had never stopped them from killing. There was a real disconnect between what they believed and how they lived.

His brother pulled him into it. By the age of twelve he had been courted in. It was an initiation to see if you could handle yourself if you ended up getting jumped by a rival gang. Four or five gang members would beat on you for three minutes and you couldn't do anything back. How that was meant to prove if you could handle yourself was a mystery. Maybe it was all about handling pain, being all macho and shit.

I couldn't help think how ridiculous it all was. I understood why people joined gangs. Those who had grown up in a family that was already part of one, or those who had nothing going for them and they were looking for some sense of belonging. But the killing for no reason, seemed pointless. At least now, we had a reason to kill. It was pure survival. We were faced with life or death situations. But back before that, there was no reason, except ego. And it was the wrong type.

Elijah showed us a photo of his family. His brother had been burnt alive by a rival gang. They had caught him off guard with his wife and two kids. Now by all accounts most gang members would let it slide if they saw you with your family. It was a sign of respect. It was the only time they would let you walk on by, however that wasn't the case for Elijah's brother. They had shot his family while he watched and then poured gasoline over him and set him on fire.

They recorded the whole thing and then sent them the flash drive in a Christmas card. In a fucking Christmas card! He had never forgotten that. That night he told us of how he discovered the ones responsible for the death of his brother and his family.

They had managed to corner the three men. What he told us next nearly made me gag. They took them out into the desert, stripped them, cut off the testicles of one of the men and made the other two eat them. They repeated it for the other two. After that they scooped out their eyeballs with spoons. All the while the men were still alive. Bleeding out, but feeling excruciating pain. When that was done they buried them in the ground near to an ants' nest and let the desert creatures eat them alive. Who knows how long they remained conscious. It no longer mattered. To Elijah he had vindicated his brother's murder.

And yet as he told us this, he said something very profound. Elijah thought he would feel better afterward, and for a brief moment he did. Then the satisfaction was gone. All he could feel was numb. He realized that he had become like them. No better.

He didn't say it. But the look in his eyes was enough. If given the opportunity, he wanted out from the gang life. But what could he do? There was nothing else he knew. As atrocious as it was, gang life was all he had.

Elijah led us out that morning after breakfast. He brought with him six other guys. He wasn't taking any chances. They had been experiencing a number of attacks by the Reapers. While they had managed to secure off the area around the cinema, Elijah felt it was only a matter of time before the Reapers would try to take that as well.

Not much had changed since the apocalypse for them. It was still about territory, respect, and being the baddest motherfuckers on the streets. To us it seemed meaningless. To them, it was everything. Gang banging, dealing, robbing stores, and putting a cap in the enemy was still at the top of their agenda.

They took us as far as they could before turning back. They knew the areas where their rival gangs went. It would have been insane for them to cross over into that section of the neighborhood without more of their homies. I thanked Elijah and wished him the best of luck. I had a sense that he saw something in our group that he connected with. What it was? I was unsure about that but he definitely looked disconnected from his group that morning.

When we parted ways, it would take us close to twenty minutes to haul ass over to the CDC. Elijah had given us a clear route out of the city for after. A path that would keep us clear of the Reapers and other gangs. Instead, we wanted to check out the CDC before we left. I guess we still held out some smidgen of hope that whoever had broadcast that signal, was still around, or at least had left directions to a safe zone.

"So what do you think this safe zone will be like?" Specs asked.

"I'm hoping it's a harem of women, booze, marijuana, and Pop-Tarts," Baja replied while keeping an eye on the rooftops. Truth be told, none of us had really given much thought to what it would be like. Anything had to be an improvement over our current situation. Personally I had envisioned a section of suburbs walled off from the rest of society, where remaining troops had pitched up camp and guarded the walls day and night. Dax believed it would be a camp run by FEMA. Basically a massive prison complex that would house anyone not infected.

"Dax, you got to be out of your mind. A prison?"

"You think they are going to just let everyone do whatever the fuck they want? It would be anarchy," he said, casting a nervous glance around as we moved closer to Washington Square Park.

"A concentration camp? Now if they allow conjugal

library."

"Damn, I always wanted to see that place," said Specs.

"Dude, it's a library."

"No, that ain't no library, it's a work of art." I had no clue what he was on about but then again I didn't read as much as Specs did. If his nose wasn't in a book, he was building some weird contraption. Usually it was for his father. The very thought of his dad, made me sigh. We could never go back to Castle Rock. All the people we loved. It was gone.

Life would never be the same.

We stayed low and moved quietly behind vehicles until we reached 300 East Street. We hung a left and continued on our way.

As we got closer to Salt Lake Public Library on our right, I had to admit it was something to behold. The first thing we noticed was the crescent stone wall that swept around the north and east side. The whole structure was one part stone, two parts curved glass. With a five-story walkable wall and high-UV glass, it was literally shaped like a huge wedge. Dax wanted to keep going but Specs bugged him to take a few minutes and check it out. He eventually caved in.

"It's meant to store over five hundred thousand books," Specs said, staring at it in awe.

Baja sniffed. "Dude, I have more than that on my iPhone."

"You think Z's are inside?" Jess asked.

"Probably a shit load. I don't feel good about this, Johnny," Dax said.

"Settle down. You'll be in and out in five minutes, I replied.

"Yeah, Dax, you should be used to that," Izzy added.

We all stifled a laugh while Dax went a slight shade of red. The closer we got the bigger it looked. "It's like the Colosseum in Rome," I said. Small green trees were dotted around the outside, along with a fountain that ran down stone steps. Sections of it reminded me of what

Rome might have looked like in modern times. As we ascended the stone steps that led up to the entrance, we could see that multiple doors were no longer there. Blood covered them. The glass had been shattered, and some of them had been torn off the framework. We knifed a few Z's on the way in. Unless it was critical, we didn't use bullets.

Glass crunched beneath our feet as we stepped inside. High above us was a massive skylight. Multiple elevators to our right were no longer in service. One of them was completely covered in blood as if multiple people had been attacked inside of it.

There was a large sign giving an outlined map of the entire place. Stores were positioned against the stone wall to our left. In the atrium to our right was a hair salon, gift stores, a flower shop, an art gallery, and multiple cafés. Tables and chairs had been overturned. The floors were littered and smeared red. Decaying bodies were laid out from brutal attacks though some looked as if people had jumped to their deaths. Did they have no other option?

With every new place I entered, I would momentarily close my eyes and envision what had taken place. What were the horrors witnessed by young children as adults turned on each other and the once peaceful place became a scene of terror?

I diverted my eyes from two young children whose faces had been eaten. A stroller lay on its side empty but covered in blood.

It would have been foolish to think the place was clear. It must have been filled with Z's. While most weren't on the ground, we could hear the snarling and moans on the four floors above us. Izzy jumped back as a Z toppled over the edge of a balcony. We didn't even hear it coming, just the splat as it hit the granite floor in front of us.

"Have we seen enough?"

Even Baja was shaking his head in disbelief.

"Come on, let's go up," Specs said.

"You've got to be joking, Specs. We're not going up

there," Dax shot back.

"You know something, Dax. If you don't want to go, then fuck you. Go on with your mission to find this dumb ass signal. You think you are going to find it in this city? I have given myself time and time again to help you all. Now, I'm asking for one time. One damn time, to check out a few things and you want to deny me that? Screw you."

And with that Specs went off by himself.

Dax was as surprised as all of us. Specs wasn't someone who got irate easily. Maybe the days were beginning to take a toll on him. But he just snapped in that moment.

It wasn't like we needed supplies, or ammo immediately. We had come to the city with a purpose, and nowhere in that was risking our lives to go sightseeing. Yet, we all knew that we might not see tomorrow. With that in mind, and because I think Dax actually thought the kid had balls, Dax followed him up. What we didn't know was the danger that we would face next, would far exceed those that came back from the dead.

COMMANDER-IN-CHIEF

They were encircled when we came across them. Dax had pulled me back. He wanted to assess the situation. We were on the third floor. Each of us was laid out in various spots with our assault rifles on the ready.

We didn't think anyone was going to walk in, let alone someone of real significance. Prior to their arrival, we had been at the library for close to thirty minutes before the drama unfolded. We used the winding stairs to get up to the different levels above us. It was full of shelves, glass walls, curved canopies above, and high-tech designs. Everything about the place screamed modern architecture. People who had more money than sense. It was just a library for God's sake; a fancy one, but nothing more than that. Fuck knows what Specs's fascination was with the place. I enjoyed a library as much as anyone else, but that was before we were overrun with the dead looking to take a chunk out of our ass.

We figured the place was filled with Z's by the noise that came from the ground floor, but it was just the echo that made it sound like there were more. Each level had close to twenty of the ugly brutes. A few were fast-moving ape types that shuffled on all fours towards us. We soon slammed their brakes on with a cap in the head. Ten minutes later we had cleared the rest with knives. I'd like to say we were getting used to hacking our way through this new world, but you didn't get used to it. You couldn't. Every time I drove a blade into a mangled face of a monster, I couldn't help but wonder who they were, how they died, and what had become of their own kin. Sometimes I didn't have the luxury of thinking about it in the heat of the moment. Most often the thoughts came late at night, when I closed my eyes.

It was then I would see their faces. Eventually they just blurred into one image. It had got to the point that I kept seeing myself pressed against a wall, fighting one and using nothing but my hands to tear its head from its shoulders.

Was killing them changing us? It had to be. Hours of fear and adrenaline spiking in our systems, repeating over and over. This must have been how our ancestors lived before the dinosaurs were wiped out. Could these monsters ever be wiped out?

Below, six men in their late twenties toyed with their victims like wolves rounding up prey.

The prey? Initially there were two men in dark suits until they put a bullet in the head of one of them. The other pushed what looked like an eighteen-year-old brunette behind his back as they cornered them. He laid his gun down and slid it across the floor, hoping to avoid the same fate. Instead they began a violent beating. Kicking him from all angles as he balled up. Then, tossing him between them like a rag doll. While four found pleasure inflicting brutal punishment on him, the others laughed as they tore at the girl's blouse exposing her bra.

"This is not right," I said.

A Hispanic guy wearing khakis, an oversized white T-shirt, and a pair of Chuck Taylors pawed at the girl's breasts as Dax pulled me back. All of them wore blue bandanas, identifying them as Reapers. Grim Reapers.

Keeping his voice low, he spoke, "We can't get involved, Johnny. We don't know how many more of them there are."

"You want to let her get raped?"

Dax ground his teeth.

"No, but I don't want to get caught up in a gang war either."

"I don't think we have a choice."

I went to get up, and he grabbed me by the collar. "If you do this, they all die. You want that on your conscience?" I paused, glaring at him for a moment and allowing the thought to linger before pushing him away.

I motioned for the others to come close. Baja, Specs, and I were going down. The others would provide additional cover from above, especially if any of them tried to bolt. At the bottom we would give them the signal. Staying low as we descended, we hugged the inside of the staircase. Once our boots hit the ground floor, we moved quietly in the direction of the men, fanning out and using stone pillars as cover.

"I want her first," one of them shouted.

Another shoved him back. "Fuck you. This gash is mine."

They turned over a table, hiked up her skirt, and bent her over. The girl was screaming as one tried to control her arms while another began unbuckling his belt. These weren't the type of men that would negotiate, neither would they run from a fight. I looked up and signaled to the others with a closed fist.

It was over in a matter of seconds.

Round after round was unleashed until each of the six dropped.

The girl immediately hurried over to the man that was still alive but badly beaten. She gripped him tight. Her eyes scanned up and down, back and forth like a petrified animal.

"It's alright, we're not going to harm you," I said.

I swung my assault rifle to my side and with my hands out moved towards her. She squeezed her eyes tight instinctively as if expecting the worst. Meanwhile Baja and Specs went over and checked that the six were dead. Satisfied, they removed their handguns. The others above joined us on the ground floor.

She was visibly shaken but when she saw Jess and Izzy her breathing began to slow. It was if by the very fact that other women were okay, she must have figured she wouldn't be hurt.

"Please. Help him," she said.

"Ralphie, Dax, take him up."

"Are we gonna stay here?" Ralphie asked.

"Just for the night."

We had a small med kit on us that we had obtained from Benjamin. It was packed with everything you would need to treat basic to pretty extreme wounds and snake bites; gauze bandages, antiseptic wipes, safety pins, dressing for major wounds, quick clot, alcohol, different types of pills, plastic bags for waste, shears, a thermometer, EDC kit, a tourniquet, and a whole whack load of antibiotic creams and shit. It would have made Specs's father proud.

While they were taking care of him Jess and Izzy led the girl up. Over the next five minutes we dragged the bodies into a store that been broken into. It was a café. If there were more Reapers out there, we didn't want them to see their fallen brothers. Specs made sure they weren't going to make any comeback by pushing a blade into their skulls.

On our way out we snagged up a can of coffee, and a few bags of cookies we found inside a storeroom.

"Should we find something to push up against the doors?"

There were four double doors at the front entrance, all of them were glass, one of them had been smashed in, another torn off its hinges. We couldn't exactly keep anyone out, but we could make it a little difficult for them to sneak up on us in the night. We searched around for something to tie off the doors from the inside, and then dragged over a bunch of tables and chairs and stacked them on top of each other outside and inside. Again, we knew if someone wanted to get in badly enough they could. But they were going to make one hell of a noise. It just had to work for the night.

After we were done, we joined the others up on the fifth floor.

* * *

Maybe it was the heat of the moment, or fear, but none of us except Specs seemed to recognize who the girl was, when he told me I stopped in my tracks. She was the president's daughter, Kat Greer.

"You're joking?"

"No, I'm pretty certain," Specs replied.

There had been a recent change in power. A new one had come into office three months before the shit had hit the fan. We hadn't exactly paid attention. Politics had a place next to religion in our household. It was rarely discussed and when it was, it usually came out with a few f-bombs. I scoffed, remembering the way my father would speak about government.

"They are all good-for-nothings. People cheer them in and then tear them down the next day. They promise the world and deliver fuck all. It's all one big game, and one I don't intend to play."

He had the same sentiment about anyone who tried to control him, or tell him what to do. I couldn't help see the irony in it, being as he had spent the largest chunk of his life in the military. An organization where you were paid to jump, run, and shit when commanded. It was why I had no inclination to follow in his footsteps. I was no number. And I definitely wasn't going to risk my ass in the field just to keep the suits in Washington happy.

For hours Kat didn't say much. We talked among ourselves while Dax tended to his wounds. It was mostly bruises and cuts, possibly a fractured rib. We used cushions from chairs to create makeshift beds to make them comfortable. It would take some time before we would find out how they ended up there. Kat Greer stayed close to Garret who we soon learned was on presidential detail for the Secret Service.

"So we'll rotate through the night. Just two awake, and then change over after two hours."

Specs and I took the first shift. If libraries were quiet when people were in them, the place had an almost eerie feeling at night. You could have heard a pin drop. As the inside of the library had an open concept, from the top floor you could see right out across the city. Above us was a skylight. Through it, it looked like a million tiny fireflies flicking on and off in the darkness. We rested against the ledge and occasionally looked down at the main doors. The rest of the time we gazed out across the city which would have looked beautiful at night if there had been power. Instead all we could see were flames flickering from various buildings. Occasionally we would spot a light flick on then off. There had to be more people out there. Those that weren't gangs. People who had hunkered down in apartments like Benjamin. City folk who were doing their best to survive.

Specs lit a cigarette. We didn't have many left. A pack and a half. The leftovers from what we had scavenged.

"My father would say there would come a time when something like this would happen. I never quite believed him," Specs snorted.

"Isn't that always the way? We buy insurance to cover for the worst, but we never think about the world going to shit."

"Do you remember that time when the power went out in the town for six hours? How everyone started panicking — buying up water, food and talking as though the world had come to an end?" Specs said.

"Yeah. How could I forget, my old man wouldn't shut up about why the gas pumps weren't working and if the power didn't come on, we'd lose a shit load of meat that he had in the freezer. He then drank his way through an entire bottle of Jack D."

I started mimicking my father stumbling around with a bottle in hand. "'*I know the fucking government is behind this, well, you can suck my balls, Uncle Sam, you're not going to starve me out. I'll see you in hell. Hoorah!* Then he collapsed."

We both chuckled.

"Good times," we both muttered.

"Then there was my father who was as a cool as ice," Specs took a deep drag. I watched it glow a deep orange in the darkness before he handed it to me. He blew out smoke rings and I watched them disappear.

"He kicked on the generator and we just carried on as though nothing had happened. I told him he should offer people a hand. The look he gave me, I still remember it today. It was one of those, '*are you out of your friggin' mind*' kind of stares."

"Well, he did take a lot of flak from folks in the town prior to that day. You'd think everyone would have learned from that. Did they? Hell no."

Specs continued. "Meanwhile people were running around like chickens with their heads lopped off. I could never understand it. They bought insurance for property, bought vitamins to safeguard their health, and made arrangements for where their wealth would go, but no one thinks about floods, earthquakes, tornadoes, a chemical war…"

"A zombie apocalypse?" I added, blowing out smoke.

Specs chuckled. "Yeah, I know it's nuts, who would have thought that the worst thing to hit planet Earth would be our own version of Hungry Hippos."

I stretched out my aching muscles.

"So what do you make of this?"

"I dunno. It's odd for sure. Hopefully we'll get some answers tomorrow."

"If she's in Salt Lake, you think the commander-in-chief is?"

"Wouldn't that be something? Not that I think it would matter now. Who the hell is going to listen to him anyway?"

"Who listened to him before this?" Specs said.

"True. True," I said.

There was a long pause.

"Makes you think."

"About what?"

"How many can say they have seen the president's daughter's tits?"

I put my finger up to my lips. "Dude, keep it down." I cast a glance around. It was just like Specs to toss that one in there. He had no off switch. I tapped him on the arm.

"Right. Yeah, sorry about that." Then he continued. "But you got to admit it. They were beauties."

I snorted, then nodded reluctantly, feeling guilty.

"You know, I always thought the Secret Service was badass. Like, trained to take down ten men with one bullet, or break arms while tossing a salad."

"Specs, you've been watching too many Stallone movies."

"No, but didn't you? If that had been me I would have gone out in a blaze of glory shooting like the other guy did."

"Yeah, and you'd be a real help to Kat."

"But that's what these guys live for. Dying a warrior and shit. The whole, I was born to take the bullet crap."

"You buy into that?" I asked.

"Don't you?"

"Shit no. Is anything as good as it looks? The first time you fuck, the first cigarette you have, the vacation on the beach. Nah. There is always some prick who comes along and fucks it all up. Die a warrior? For what? Some medal you are never going to wear?"

"But your family will know you earned it."

"Specs," I turned to him. "Do you really think that your family is going to give a shit about a chunk of metal? They would trade a million medals for one day with their kid. So no, I don't buy the whole die like a warrior shit. I believe in making your life count. But doing it because you want to do it. Not because you give a shit about what the guy over there thinks is cool. That guy is the same one that will be crying for his mother when the mortars are flying over his head, or running for the bulletproof SUV when the gunman on the hill is snapping at his shit."

We stood in silence for a minute or two.

"You think if Arnie and Stallone had a fight Arnie would win?"

I just shook my head and smiled. Despite all that had gone bad, that was one thing that hadn't changed.

UP SHIT CREEK

There were no safe zones. Whoever had sent out the signal must have believed that the military were about to establish areas that would be beyond the reach of the dead.

They were wrong.

I breathed in deeply, looking out across a city that lay in ruin. A bright orange sun peeked over the horizon, bringing a warm band of light that chased away a long night. Smoke rose between the buildings in the distance. Were people burning the dead? Trying to stay warm? Or had they failed to escape and suffered an even worse fate?

Standing on the ledge of Salt Lake City Public Library I reflected on what Garret had told me that morning. It still hadn't sunk in. So far, no one else knew. Most were still asleep when he began to talk. They would soon realize and each one would take the news in different ways. We had got our hopes up. Believed that the city would be a safe haven. How gullible were we? And the worst was about to be made known.

The night before as we rotated shifts, I picked up a second one simply because I couldn't stop my mind from racing. Even though we had eradicated the dead inside the library, they lived on in our minds, terrorizing us as we closed our eyes. Tiredness would soon catch up with me. It always did.

Garret had joined me that morning out on the roof.

"Like I said, I know it's not the news you were hoping for, but it's something."

He had told me that the only place he knew would hold its ground was NORAD located in the Cheyenne Mountains of Colorado.

"And you? How did you come to be here?" I asked.

Garret groaned a little, taking a seat. He kicked at the graveled roof, and tossed a few small stones at a metal air vent. "I've been in the Secret Service for the past twelve years. I've seen all manner of threats on the president's life but none that topped this. It should have been a simple in and out visit. No longer than twenty-four hours. Three weeks ago, Air Force One landed at Hill Air Force Base. President Greer was visiting to speak about the economy. Well, that's all the media knew. What had not been mentioned was that another visit was added to his itinerary. One to the Centers for Disease Control."

I turned around. "You knew this was coming?"

"Look, believe it or not, it was under control at the Dugway Proving Ground in Utah."

"The Dugway? What the hell is that?"

"A military facility that tests biological and chemical weapons."

I stared, unable to comprehend what I was hearing.

"Are you telling me we created this?"

"It was a mistake," he shot back as if sensing that he was somehow to blame.

I scoffed at his response. "Yeah, I kind of figured

that much. What is it?"

"I'm no scientist. But I'm certain it was something to do with a biological weapon the military was working on."

I shook my head. "So if it was under control, how did it get out?"

"That's the part I don't know."

"What the fuck do you know?" I replied, frustrated by his lack of clarity.

"Settle down."

"Settle down? I lost my father, my friend, and so have they! Settle down?" I raised my voice, scowling at the only person I could direct my anger toward. The only one who represented government, even if he played no role in the creation of the virus.

"Listen, all I can tell you is what I learned from a scientist before he died. Spores were prematurely shipped out to eighty-eight labs in the U.S. and seven other countries. Who authorized it? Not even they knew. It was major fuckup."

"A fuckup?" I laughed. "Holy shit!" I ran a hand through my hair, trying to grab hold of the enormity of the situation. This wasn't just about a few cities, or a town being infected. We were looking at an outbreak that had gone global.

"Once they realized what it did to the human body." He paused and swallowed hard. "The CDC and Salt Lake City Laboratories began work on a possible cure. A search for an anti-virus was underway. They believed they had it.

Along with the president was a group of scientists who were going to return the sample to NORAD so that further tests could be run. Until that point, as far as we knew, the threat was minimal. It had been contained. How the infected escaped is still a mystery to us. Everything happened so fast. When all hell broke loose in the city, the first priority was the safety of the president. Under normal circumstances it wouldn't have been a problem. We usually had the support of local police to escort us, but this wasn't normal. They had their hands filled, as did we. It was total chaos. As the dead started attacking, things spiraled out of control fast."

"Not that it matters, but the president, where is he?"

Garret's eyes dropped. "I'm not… exactly sure. Dead, maybe."

It felt like the world around me was caving in.

"Unbelievable," I said, pacing back and forth.

He let out a sigh, squeezed his eyes shut as if trying to recall. "Initially we were all together, we remained inside the hotel waiting for a team to come in and extract him."

"And if they can't?"

"Everything is already planned and mitigated in the event of his death or inability to perform his duties."

"A transfer of power to the vice president and then the next idiot, though that wouldn't happen if there was no one alive to transfer it to, would it?" I muttered.

"Right, and as far as we knew others were still alive. But then things got even worse. We soon got word that

Hill Air Force Base was overrun, and Air Force One had been destroyed. Those that had managed to get out in time said they would send someone to extract the president. No one came. We were on our own. Myself, six others from the Secret Service, two scientists, and his daughter, Kat."

"Forgive me while I shed a tear," I said shaking my head.

Garret ran a hand over his tired face.

"Anyway, as the days went by it just got worse. No one showed up. The hotel was on lockdown to prevent the dead for getting in, and yet they still managed to find entry. When the power went down, we knew we had to get out. Three of the agents escorted the scientists out first. We made it to the stairwell before we were forced back into the room. Only one of them returned. A scientist. His leg had been bitten."

He paused trying to compose himself. I could see the fear in his eyes as he recalled what had led up to this moment.

He continued. "Behind the door we could hear the sound of the dead trying to get in. I'll never forget it. It was so loud. It wouldn't stop. At one point I just covered my ears. Then survival instincts kicked in and we moved the president to the roof using a fire escape. Over a period of two days we remained there exposed to the elements until the real animals arrived."

"Real animals?"

"The gang you saw last night. They had spotted us from another building. Initially they had pretended to be hotel workers. We couldn't see them on the other side of the door. They said they would die if we didn't open. What were we meant to do? I didn't want to open. The president made the call in the end. Big mistake. They outnumbered us the moment we opened it."

"You blame yourself for it?"

He fixed his gaze on me. "Not once has the president been hurt under my watch."

"So how did you get away?"

He was about to tell me when Jess joined us.

"There you are. I was wondering where you'd gone. Dax and the others are up."

"We'll be there in a moment."

Jess nodded, her eyes darting between the two of us.

"Is Kat okay?" Garret asked.

"Yeah. Still shaken up, but as well as can be."

Jess could tell she had interrupted our conversation. She gestured that she was leaving and then disappeared back down the steps. Garret looked out across the city, shaking his head.

"Even with the best military in the world and we still lost control."

I prompted him to continue. "You were saying?"

He glanced at me, squinting as if trying to regain his train of thought. "They stopped to siphon gas, we took advantage of the moment, overpowered the two watching over us. I grabbed Kat and we bolted. We lost another guy trying to escape."

"And the president?"

"He was in a different vehicle. There was no way we could have got to him."

"Where were they taking you?"

"I heard them say something about Temple Square."

I blew out my cheeks, registering it.

Garret must have noticed. "You know what's there?"

"Grim Reapers. We met up with one of their rival gangs. They had told us they had taken it over."

Garret nodded. "I heard them talking about someone who went by the name Domino."

"Their leader," I replied.

Garret tossed a stone over the edge and watched it drop.

"Why didn't you just leave the city?" I asked.

"Because that's not my mission. My job is to make sure the president is safely returned."

"Kind of late for that, isn't it?"

"Until I know any different, he's still alive."

"Even if he is, and you could get him out, where would you take him?"

"NORAD. That's where they'll be."

"Who?"

"Government. Scientists."

"And if he's dead?" I asked

"Dead or alive. It doesn't matter, at least to society. But what he's carrying — that's important."

"Which is?"

"The cure."

My eyes grew wide.

"There's really a cure for this shit?" Dax's voice came from behind us.

I glanced over my shoulder to see him walking towards us.

Garret directed his answer to him. "If the scientist from the CDC was right — yeah. They had created a sample that tested positive for destroying the virus."

"Well, you can kiss that goodbye. If he had it on him, the Reapers have it now."

“No. It’s a storage device embedded in the president. They wouldn’t know.”

“I don’t believe you,” I said. “Why would they inject a sample into the president? His job is to stay alive, not to be placed at risk. After the screw-up they had with those spores, hell, the Secret Service wouldn’t have allowed it, let alone him.”

“We didn’t allow it. And they didn’t inject it. He did.”

“What?” Dax asked with a look of complete disbelief.

“The moment things started to spiral out of control. Before we lost the last scientist, it was given to him. He wasn’t prepared to let it fall into the wrong hands. He chose to inject the small device into the corner of his hip.”

“And that’s not dangerous?”

“No, the test sample is contained within a fully sealed titanium device.”

“Ok, but why inject it? If it’s just a sample, it would

be useless to anyone."

"Can you imagine what that would be worth in the wrong hands?"

"You think that anyone cares about money?" I paused. "News flash, Garret! There's no one left to pay for it. And money is obsolete."

"You're not seeing the bigger picture here. It's leverage. Besides, not everyone has died. They have things in place for the continuation of government. Four hundred are at NORAD, and that doesn't take into account all the other places in the USA and around the world that would be used for the continuation of life. That sample is the most valuable asset on the planet right now, and I'm not leaving without it."

I squeezed the bridge of my nose before I broke into a rant.

"You're telling me the only known possible cure that exists for this complete fuckup that was started by our own government, is inside the president of the United States? Who could be, maybe, might be… dead? Walking the streets as one of those things. Or hell, worse — holed up among two hundred Reapers! And you want to go in and get him?"

Garret paused a beat. "Yeah, that's about the extent of it."

I stared back at him, studying his face before I begun to shake my head. "You're out of your fucking mind."

Garret narrowed his eyes.

"Garret, it can't be done," Dax said.

He stared blankly back at us.

I threw up my hands and began walking away. "Fuck no, we are not getting involved."

"We're talking about the only cure for a global epidemic," Garret replied.

I came charging back. "And I'm talking about our survival."

"There won't be any survival if we don't get that sample," he spat back.

For a moment I thought about shoving him off the

roof. I don't know why I was directing my anger at him. Maybe I just needed to vent.

"Why not just go to the CDC and get another? I mean they must have had more, right?" Dax asked.

"Maybe."

"Johnny?" Dax asked.

I screwed my face up. "Hell, no. We are already up shit creek without a paddle."

With that I walked away, left the roof, and joined the others down below.

* * *

Jess immediately could tell something wasn't right. She approached me but I just shrugged it off and kept my distance. That last thing I needed now was to rehash the shit I had just heard.

I had been eager to save Millie and Caitlin back in Castle Rock. To be someone who might change the outcome for another. This wasn't Castle Rock. It wasn't my call. It wasn't our place to risk our lives. Besides, what had come from all of our help? They had got to live a few more days. A few more fucking days! I wasn't sure what I was angry with, the dead that shuffled on the streets, or the ones that had created them? They were both equally responsible for death. Yet the dead just acted on mindless instinct. The living should have known better. Creating biological weapons to kill other humans. When would we ever learn that no amount of killing led to peace? I could feel something break inside me. The thought of the military invading another country. All their macho bullshit. I couldn't blame the soldiers. They were only doing their duty. But so were those who they fought against. Back and forth. One war after the next. To what gain? A few more years of peace? Before more death? Before the assholes in Washington villainized a new target? Created a new war on terror? Had this been another one of their sick games? Playing with human life like Russian roulette. Except this time the bullet had killed us.

I was beginning to lose hope. Did it really matter if we did anything for others, if we would end up dead later?

Baja strolled over.

"You want breakfast?" he said, munching on something that looked like a turd.

"Nah."

"Think I can have yours?"

"Go ahead, man," I replied. "I've lost my appetite."

FLIP A COIN

According to Garret, the Disease Control and Prevention Center was fourteen minutes away on an ordinary day, and that was if you had a vehicle. We didn't. It was thirty by foot. To say that I was feeling a little deflated by my conversation with him would have been putting it mildly. Dax gathered the others together after breakfast to get their vote. We had already planned on going over to the CDC but that was before I found out there were no safe zones. Now it all seemed so meaningless. I could barely process what Garret had told me. I watched from a distance as the others came to the reality of our predicament. Izzy glanced at Jess. Baja made a joke of it and Specs seemed lost in thought, then again he always looked that way. Ralphie was the only one other than my brother who thought it made sense.

"Listen, we can stay here, or try to find some place to survive and live out the rest of our days, or we can be involved in getting the president back."

I know he meant well, but Ralphie was a bit of an oddball. On the surface he didn't resemble the William Wallace, let me give you a motivational speech, type of guy. More like the fella who asked if you wanted to super-size that meal. And if you did, tough shit because he had already eaten it. He wore round glasses, and some might have said he looked as though he had worked his way through his fair share of Happy Meals. Not that it mattered, we all had our vices. Mine had been cigarettes. I had been trying to kick the habit since I was twelve. When asked how I got started, I would tell people that I picked up butts that people tossed down at the bus stop, just so I could gross them out. The truth was, Specs nabbed them from his old man.

Anyway back to our Tony Robbins wannabe.

"This could be it, guys. Our chance to shine. To be all we can be."

Okay, he was starting to sound like a bloody infomercial for the army. And he may have convinced everyone if… Baja hadn't tossed a half-eaten weiner at his forehead.

"Alright, enough of that shit," Baja interrupted. "Let me cut to the chase. What our dear friend here is trying to say through the drivel that is coming out his mouth is this. If we don't go find this cure that is hidden in the president's ass—"

"Uh… it's not," Garret cut him off.

"What? Not what?" Baja snapped back.

"It's not in his ass, it's in his hip."

"Hip, ass it's all a little to near to the hole for my liking. Anyway, as I was saying before I was rudely interrupted by a member of the secret society…"

"It's Secret Service."

"Yeah, about that. Don't you think it's kind of dumb that you call yourselves the Secret Service? I mean, I know about you. Pretty much most of the United States does. It's not exactly a secret. You might wanna rethink the name, bud. Just a thought." He paused.

"Um, I'll keep that in mind." Garret looked at the others and rubbed his head as if wondering if the medications we had given him for pain were actually mind-altering drugs.

"Where was I? Oh yeah, now, we either go up against two hundred Reapers and rescue the president, or we can head over to the CDC and see if we can find another sample of the cure, and the president can go fuck himself. I vote, the president goes fuck himself. Who's with me?"

He pumped the air with his fist.

"Hey, that's my father you're talking about," Kat piped up.

"Whoa, whoa, darlin'. No need to shoot the messenger. I'm just saying. I mean let's face it. If he had actually done his job, we probably wouldn't be in this mess."

I couldn't argue with that. Her nostrils flared. At this point I would have usually intervened but Izzy did it.

"Baja, go take a nap," Izzy pushed him aside and stepped up on this chair that Ralphie had been using to give his Winston Churchill speech. She looked around at us, peered over at me. I had sat by the window, occasionally glancing over.

"There's no point blaming anyone here. What's done is done. So, I don't think anyone needs to be told what to do. We go to the CDC, see what we can find. Worst-case scenario there's nothing and we move on, or…" she paused and looked at Kat. "We offer our help."

I let out a stifled laugh. It was loud enough that Izzy heard.

"Do you have something to add, Johnny?"

"I just think it's absurd. Why should we risk our lives for someone who for all we know could be dead?"

"Uh, because he has the cure."

"You presume he has the cure. No offense…" I looked at Garret. "But we don't know that for sure."

"I told you he does," Garret replied.

"You might be convinced — we're not!" I said.

"And we have met our fair share of people who lie."

He lifted his hands. "What possible reason could I have to lie?"

"Uh, let me think. You have a so-called perfect track record of protecting the president. Maybe your ego has been battered a little. Then there is of course the glaring fact that you have his daughter with you."

Kat stood up and walked over to me. "Forget that he's the president. If it was your father, would you leave him?"

I stared at her for a moment. Her steely blue eyes bore into me, waiting for an answer.

"You never met my father. He was an asshole."

"Are you sure?" Garret said, studying my face.

"Look this isn't about me, or my father. It's about you. How many others out there have had their parents, brothers, sisters, and children stolen from them? What makes you think we give a damn?"

"Because you helped us," Kat replied. "Why did you help us? You didn't even know who we were. You could have looked the other way. Slipped out without being noticed."

I never answered; instead I just contemplated what she was asking.

"Well?"

She wasn't going to let up until I answered. I looked at the others, they too looked as if they were waiting.

I shot back. "Because it was the right thing to do!"

"And you don't think this is the right thing to do?"

I pointed at her. "There were six of them. There are two hundred Reapers."

"We can see if the Dark Kings can help," Jess added. I heaved a heavy sigh, got up, and walked away. I didn't want to get into it. They had obviously made up their minds as to what they wanted to do. This was no game. These men were killers. They wouldn't hesitate to pull the trigger. It would have been like going up against an army.

* * *

I went down a level into an area that was assigned for kids. It was amazing how they had designed the library. There were sections of the building, special rooms dedicated for kids to play in. One of them had been built like an ice cave with a skylight. I took a seat in there and looked up. Any small sound had me on edge. Every day it seemed that way. Unable to rest. The thought that we had overlooked something.

A few minutes passed before Jess came in, she looked at me and then gazed around. I knew she was there to give me some lecture about how I should help out. Instead, I was surprised to find that she didn't say anything. In fact, she never spoke a word. Maybe it was female reverse psychology but it worked. She got me speaking.

"So you want to get involved with this?"

"I'm not really sure." She cut a sideways glance. "I don't think sticking around here is much use either."

"Tell me I'm not mad, Jess, to want to avoid this?"

She came over and took a seat beside me, placing her hands behind her before gazing up at the skylight.

She breathed out. "Did I tell you that my father liked you?"

I burst out laughing. "You want me to believe that now?"

"It's true."

"Well, he had a funny way of showing it," I replied.

The first time I had turned up at her house, her father answered the door. He wasn't in uniform but he didn't need to be. He always had this intimidating presence. Something that made you feel as though he could read your mind. I guess in certain ways maybe he could. I couldn't say my thoughts towards his daughter were completely pure. But then again was any guy my age different? I think he knew that. That first day he had grilled me on the doorstep about my intentions, he then led me into his home and showed me where he kept his guns. He never said anything that made me feel as though he would have put a cap in my ass, but the message was very subtle. Fuck with my daughter, or even fuck her, and I will bring down the strong arm of the law.

I chuckled at the memory.

"He liked you because you were the only kid that had the nerve to show up twice at the door."

I stifled a laugh. "You are telling me those you dated before me never went back to the house?"

"Nope." She let out a small laugh.

"Is that why you changed your mind about going out with me?"

"I want to say you were persistent, Johnny. But no, I just pitied you." She let out a deep laugh.

"Great, thanks."

She slapped me in the gut. "I'm kidding. I dunno, maybe I felt safe around you."

I didn't know how to respond to that.

"That was then, this is now. No one is safe."

"Maybe not today, but tomorrow..." she trailed off.

That was what I liked about her. She was

optimistic. She saw hope when I couldn't. And right about then, I couldn't see it. Like tiredness hitting you after days of staying up late. I found myself being hit by a wall of doubt. I was questioning myself and everything we were doing. Surely others had done the same? They must have. We had seen it. In our journey to Salt Lake we came across those who hadn't been bitten but had taken their lives. An old couple in their abandoned trailer who had shot themselves. Guns in hand. Blood splatter behind them. Their hands interlocked with each other. I didn't like to linger in the thought of suicide. But it had crossed my mind several times since this had kicked off.

At first it was the worry of having my skin torn, and my vital organs ripped from my body. You know, what anyone might want to avoid — pain. Hell, I cried like a bitch when I had to get my tooth pulled. The dentist had to give me laughing gas not because I was scared, but because he was. I acted irrational when it came to pain. But it wasn't enduring pain that scared me, but the thought of the unknown. What did it feel like? How long would it take before I was dead? All these thoughts I pondered multiple times. All I saw was the inevitable. So forgive me, if the thought of putting a bullet through my own skull sounded selfish.

"I don't even like the president," I said.

"We're not doing it for him. Do it for others, those who need the cure."

I groaned and she quickly put it in perspective.

"Do it for yourself, your brother, or me."

I breathed out deeply. As I did she reached across and took a hold of the side of my face.

"Think about it, okay?"

"You know you are going to be the death of me," I said.

She smirked.

* * *

After checking our ammo we rolled out. We would pass right by Temple Square, unless we went the long way around which would have added another twenty minutes or so to our time. None of us wanted that.

We were like a line of ants just waiting to be stomped on. The city did little to cover us. You would think that you could move through the streets unnoticed because no one would be so out of their mind as to think about venturing out.

Nope, not these raving lunatics.

Business was as usual, except the government and city police were no longer in charge. Some of the streets had been purposely blocked. They couldn't exactly build a wall of vehicles, but they had pushed some of them into areas so they could control where Z's went. This made the whole city feel like a maze. One moment you would head down a street thinking it was going to lead you into the next, and the next moment you would have to go back the same way.

Initially Dax had wanted to have the women hang back with Ralphie and Specs but that went down real bad. Izzy got into a spitting match with him over how women could hold their own and if he didn't start showing some damn respect she was going to put a cap in his ass. Of course Specs found this hilarious, and took every chance he could to rub it in.

It was hard to say what we expected to find at the CDC. By the look on Dax's face I figured he thought there would be a team of scientists poring over the latest test samples. I certainly wasn't holding out hope. We had seen too much devastation. Ralphie led the way, which I'm sure challenged Dax's misguided superiority complex. He was used to being the head of the pack.

We moved as a tight unit. At corners Ralphie would give us the okay and one by one we would hustle across the street to the cover of the next alleyway. What probably would have made for a nice walk before the apocalypse was brutal. The closer we got to Temple Square the less we used our guns. We kind of figured Domino's men would be circling the place like guards on a prison wall. Everywhere we went the walls were either covered in blood or daubed with graffiti. Gangs placed their own tags over one another's. It was a childish insult, but they took it seriously.

"Is that what I think it is?" Baja asked, moving closer to a white 1979 Ford Country Squire station wagon with wood trim down the side. The same kind he had taken off-road on a joy ride. Its occupants must have run out of gas or left in hurry as both the driver's and passenger doors were wide open.

"Shit it is," Specs said, pausing to take a look. Baja ran his hand over it as if it were the Holy Grail. The others kept on moving.

"Guys, let's go," Jess hollered.

"There, there, baby. One day. Me and you." Baja patted the hood before joining us.

CDC

We slipped passed Temple Square without incident. Were we lucky? Perhaps. We soon discovered the reason they didn't see us was because a horde of Z's had overrun one of their armored vehicles patrolling the area. Gunfire shattered what little peace we were clinging to.

It didn't make it any better that it had begun to rain hard. The streets had turned into a stream that was soaking our clothes and making it hard to focus. We dashed through the downpour, peering around corners and setting our eyes on the next source of cover.

It wasn't the rain but the Z's that bothered us.

The sound of moans filled our ears as we rushed past the street where the armored vehicle was under attack. For once we were grateful that we weren't the ones being forced into hiding. The trouble was it could happen so fast. One minute you would be staring down five or six of them and that would soon turn into twenty, then fifty. In the city they were like rats. The streets were crawling with them.

We crouched low, weaving our way around burnt-out vehicles, sometimes seeking momentary cover inside. Which meant cozying up to some burned-up corpse. I wouldn't have wished that on my worst enemy. Every second that passed I imagined them coming to life and sinking sizzled teeth into my neck.

Passing the carnage, we saw a couple rushing through the streets with a baby. They glanced at us and for a split second they looked as if they were contemplating asking for our help; instead they turned and raced into an alleyway. No doubt they would meet a nasty fate. How many babies had been torn up? I shivered at the thought.

The strangest thing was that even though we were soaked to our skin, the rain was a welcome sight. It washed away the grime of going days without bathing in rivers or shallow ponds. Of course it made everything that much more dangerous. In the city, Benjamin had said they had to go down into the sewers to find pipes still filled with water. It was brutal, but something that you relished. I'd hoped, no, dreamed that the safe zones would have warm showers.

I had to let go of that thought. It would eat me up inside. The constant what-ifs never led to anything but depression and I couldn't afford to be depressed. In this world it would get you killed.

I slammed a machete into the forehead of a Z and stumbled over its body.

We turned the final corner that led up to the CDC. It was your typical government building. Nothing fancy, at least the one in Salt Lake City wasn't. It was a four-story building, its once light brown colors had been bleached by the rays of the sun, a large chunk of the side had been ripped away as if someone had fired a mortar into it. Brickwork had crumbled and most of its windows were shattered.

"Perhaps an explosion?" Specs asked.

"Or an attack," I said.

Dead bodies lay everywhere. This wasn't uncommon for the city. It was like a minefield, except you never quite knew if the next body you stepped over was going to take a piece out of your leg.

We moved fast.

The threat of Z's was forever at the forefront of our minds, but now we had even more to contend with. Fully armed Grim Reapers looking to get their kicks were sure to be out looking for their men who had gone missing.

Stumbling over large bricks we made our way inside.

The corridor reminded me of a hospital. It had a very sterile feel to it. I think all of us knew that it was very unlikely we were going to find anything of value inside, let alone the cure. I wouldn't have minded if it had just been a few us that had gone out, but having all of us in there. It was risky. Stupid even.

I kept my shotgun at the ready as we advanced forward. Doorways were on both sides of the corridor. There was no telling what was going to come out of them or how many Z's were inside. We crept down the first corridor without incident. Every time we turned a corner we saw more lifeless bodies. Some of them you couldn't even recognize as their faces had been chewed away. A few twitched on the floor. Those that appeared to show any sign of being a threat were quickly dealt with by me or the others.

"Do you know where you're going?" Dax asked Garret.

"Kind of. We didn't come in this way. We were taken to a lab on the lower floor."

We continued following his lead. The whole place felt eerie. We were witnessing the aftermath of a mass genocide. We passed by a room labeled EOC, Garret told us it was their Emergency Operation Center. It was dedicated to tracking and monitoring outbreaks around the world. It reminded me of a school classroom, except a lot bigger. There were lines of computers, some untouched, others scattered on the floor among dead bodies.

We cleared our way through about ten Z's before taking the stairwell down to the next floor. With more of us packing it was getting easier to move forward. I hung back at the top of the stairwell to keep watch on anyone following us. Ralphie was with me.

"I know you don't like this," Ralphie said. "But if there is even just a slim chance it's worth it."

"Maybe."

"Guys." Izzy called up to us, I peered over the stairwell. "Dax wants you to hold the position and keep an eye out."

I gave her the thumbs-up.

We heard her saying the same to Jess and Specs who were one floor below us. We stood either side of the door looking down the corridors. The sound of moaning was a constant. Where it was coming from was hard to tell. Most of the doors were locked. The only way you could get into them was with a key code, or a swipe card.

"So tell me." I cast a glance to my side. "What did you do before this?"

He looked as if he was a few years older than me.

"I worked at 7-Eleven," Ralphie replied.

"Working your way through college?"

"Nope. That was it."

I looked back. "Right, but you must have had some goal. Something you wanted to do with your life? I mean back at the library you had a lot to say. I thought you might have been a motivational speaker?"

He chuckled. "Nah, I just listened to a lot of motivation audios. Computers were my thing. Networking, hacking."

I raised my eyebrows. "Hacking?"

"Small stuff, websites, the odd government facility."

"Oh, you sly dog."

He grinned.

I scanned the rooms that I could see into. I saw a few Z's shuffling around. There wasn't any chance of them getting out so I wasn't worried. One of them looked as if his ears had been chewed off, and an eyeball was hanging by a loose muscle.

"I don't get it. You listen to all the motivational speeches, you say you're a bit of whiz with computers and yet you work at 7-Eleven?"

"It's a job," he replied.

"I know. Someone's gotta do it. But I just imagined anyone who worked there was either the owner's kid, in college, or doing a favor for a buddy. I mean how often do you see the same guy or gal down at your local convenience store? The turnover must be crazy."

"I held it down for four years," Ralphie chuckled. "That was my full-time gig. Pretty sad, isn't it?"

"Well, look it this way, you might not have managed to become president, but you're on your way to save him. I think that's a pretty sweet deal."

He nodded. "Yeah. Yeah, it is."

I only said it to cheer him up. The very mention of what he did before only seemed to dampen his spirits. It was if talking about it made him remember who he really was and being with us gave him purpose. Perhaps he was trying to break out of that mold, become something he'd never been?

Suddenly gunfire erupted below us. I shouldered the door and craned over the stairwell.

"What's going on?" I yelled.

There was no reply. All that could be heard was the echo of guns. Ralphie and I double-timed it down two flights of stairs to find Jess and Specs wrestling with Z's. Neither of us hesitated. I stabbed two of them in the side of the temple sending black gunk all over Jess's face. As I slid on blood in the hallway I could clearly see what was happening.

There must have been a hundred skin-eaters shuffling forward.

Dax, Baja, Izzy, and Garret had formed a line and were taking them down in droves but it was useless, there were too many. Sandwiched between them and us was Kat. She looked terrified. She held a gun in her hand but clearly had never used one.

The entire corridor was like a fucking slip and slide of blood and guts. The smell was like heating up an old man's cock in a microwave, and sprinkling shit all over it. I leapt up only to find myself back on my ass as a Z lunged at me. There I was trying to wrestle with a zombie version of Kojak while trying to keep an eye on Kat. I turned back to find flesh dangling against my lips. I spat and pushed the Z back. At first I thought it was part of his mouth, but then I realized, it was an eyeball hanging out. The fucking thing landed on my face.

I didn't have a chance to go for my knife as the Z had knocked it out of my hand when I landed. So I did the next best thing and took a hold of its head and slammed it three times against the wall until it crushed. Still laid back underneath a mutilated Humpty Dumpty who now had a cracked melon, I tried pushing him off but he had to have weighed a good three hundred pounds. All I could do was watch helplessly as a Z burst out of a side door at Kat.

"Specs," I bellowed.

Specs turned on a dime and fired off two rounds, not thinking for a second whether or not he was going to hit Kat. The Z spun in midair. Kat had now reached a new level of trauma as blood splattered all over her. A quick hand from Ralphie and Specs and I was back up on my feet, wiping off molasses-thick blood.

"Go, get her out," Garret was yelling. Garret had only turned for a few seconds when a Z sank its teeth into his arm. He screamed in agony and used his other to shoot it in the face. But it was too late. He'd been bitten. I grabbed Kat and we all raced into the stairwell and ascended the stairs two at a time. There was nothing to hold back the doors. The swarm of the dead followed us, some spilled over the banister as they forged towards us.

When we reached the main floor my legs were burning. My chest was on fire from breathing hard. We didn't stop or look back. The only thought pushing through my mind was to get out. To get as far away from the building as we could. We stumbled out into the rain, defeated by the dead, and for what? We had nothing, or at least that's what I thought.

We trudged our way down the street searching for the nearest abandoned building. The choice was endless. The irony was, we settled on a 7-Eleven beside a gas station.

Ralphie grinned, feeling at home. I was just glad to get out of the rain. We piled into the store, Baja and I made sure there was no one there before we locked the door behind us. The last thing we needed was any more surprises.

Garret was in agony. The Z had torn through the muscle in his right forearm. In all the confusion, someone had left the medic kit behind at the library. He was now bleeding out.

"I'll find something to tie it off," I said.

"No. Cut it," he yelled.

"What?"

"Cut it. Do it now."

We stared at each other. Dax didn't pause, blink, or

ask if he was sure. He reached a hand behind his back and in one smooth motion pulled the machete from its sheath.

"Hold him down," he said.

Baja was the only one that had presence of mind to follow his directions. Garret held out his chewed-up arm and Dax brought the blade down about ten inches up from the bite without any hesitation. More blood splatter hit Kat in the face. Some of it went in her mouth. Her eyes went as wide as dollar coins. She looked if she was in shock. Her skin was pale and body unflinching to the horror taking place before her.

Dax brought the blade down on Garret's arm four times before he cut through the bone. Garret went unconscious from pain in two. We stood there staring at the severed arm in a pool of blood while Dax tied off the stump with his own pant belt.

"You think that will do it?" Jess asked.

"No. But it's all we've got for now. We need to cauterize it fast to stop the bleeding."

Without any power, all we had was a BIC lighter that Baja pulled out.

"Yeah, this isn't a concert, you moron. I'm pretty sure we are going to need something bigger than that," Dax said.

Specs got up and began looking around. He disappeared down an aisle. We could hear him rooting through the little that remained in the store.

"Here we go," he came back with some TRESemmé hairspray.

"I don't think he needs a new hairdo, dude," Baja replied.

Specs shook his head and took the lighter.

"Stand back."

He placed the lighter in front of the travel canister. It couldn't have been much bigger than his hand. He flicked it on and a flame appeared. A quick burst of hairspray and a flame shot out a foot long.

"By the way I hear that's all the rage now. Using swords and fire to cut hair."

"Baja, I swear you are demented," Izzy said, watching in horror.

"No, I'm dead serious. I saw it on TV. Some Aussie was slicing the shit out of some chick's hair and burning the ends with fire."

"I'll remember that when I need a haircut, now can we get his arm sorted out?"

Specs was already on it. Everyone averted their eyes at the sound of sizzling flesh. The smell was far worse than we imagined. It reeked of rotten eggs and weeks-old milk. When Specs pulled back I glanced at his handiwork. I wasn't sure what I was expecting to see. But it wasn't that. He had practically turned the guy's stub into a roasted sausage. I'd seen marshmallows on the end of a stick fare better at a campfire than that. But at least it wasn't bleeding. I grimaced at the sight. Garret had remained unconscious through it all, though I figured if he had woken up he would have probably passed out.

"Kat."

She stared forward barely blinking.

"Kat," I repeated.

I got up and went over to Dax who was admiring Specs's handiwork. I grabbed him by the arm and pulled him into an aisle.

"Was that trip worth it? Did you find anything? I told you we shouldn't have gone."

"Get your hand off me, Johnny."

I glared at him and slowly released my grip.

"You want to blame me for that? Really? After some of the shit you pulled back at home?"

I looked away.

"Yeah, I thought so."

"Things aren't going to go right, Johnny. You know that. Every day we walk out there, there is a chance that you, me, or one of them isn't coming back. If you have a problem with that, you need to deal with it now. This is war, brother. No matter how you look at it. We are up against an enemy that has us outnumbered. The odds of us surviving are very fucking slim. So buckle up, grow some balls and help, or stay the fuck out of my way."

Silence ensued for a moment as both of us sat in the discomfort of our own words.

"And as for what we found. Yeah, it was worth it. We didn't find the cure if that's what you're asking. But Garret found this!"

Dax pulled from a leather bag what looked like a communications unit.

"I think we can use this."

"Is that military?" I asked.

"It doesn't look like what I've seen in the field," he replied. "But maybe the military tried to pull employees out of the CDC when this happened?"

"More like attacked them," Kat mumbled. She didn't turn our way.

"Kat. Do you know something about what went down at the CDC?"

She craned her head around. "I know that the military wasn't taking any chances on who was infected. We saw them killing regular people. They slaughtered them like cattle."

I glanced at Dax. "You still want to use that?"

7-ELEVEN

The 7-Eleven had three aisles of shelving and a cooler at the back. The ground was tiled white with a thick streak of blood that went out back. Whatever had been killed had got up and walked away or been devoured. What struck us as strange was that while the place had clearly been ransacked, not everything had been taken. A few cartons of milk that had expired weeks ago were still in there. None of us was brave enough to drink it especially after Baja stuck it under our noses. And I thought Z's smelled bad! A rotisserie hotdog machine still had hotdogs. Cold and with a good amount of mold. I forced myself to taste one to the laughter of everyone. They tasted like shit even when there wasn't a zombie apocalypse and because they were still there, we assumed others thought the same. It was the one thing you didn't touch even if you were starving. That stuff could give you indigestion like no other food. I had once bought one of their burgers in a cardboard box just to see how bad they were. I'm pretty sure I used it for a doorstop. The thing was solid. The guy behind the counter wouldn't give me my money back. "No returns," he said in a thick Indian accent, followed up with, "Do you want to buy a Lotto ticket?"

I flipped him the bird.

We had been in there for close to six hours. It was the middle of the afternoon. We had pushed some of the shelving in front of the doors and used some loose rope behind the counter to tie off the handles. Our worry wasn't as much Z's breaking in, as it was the Grim Reapers.

Garret didn't look as if he was improving. All the color had run from his face. He was sweating profusely and showing signs that I had seen in Caitlin before she turned. Dax was berating himself for waiting so long to chop off the arm. I could hear him muttering about cutting higher, cutting sooner, cutting cleaner. I don't think it really mattered. We had no clue if a person could survive if a leg or arm was cut off. Did the virus or whatever the hell this was move through the system immediately? Or was it slow? By the time we had made it to the 7-Eleven, Garret had already lost a lot of blood. If he didn't bleed to death, he would eventually turn.

I turned to find Baja with his head under the slushy machine draining what remaining drops it would release without power. Specs flipped through a porn magazine and had his head tilted to one side to see the center spread. Ralphie stared absently up at an employee of the month photo, probably reassessing his life goals. I ventured out back to see what I could scavenge. When we had initially entered and cleared the rooms, I'd seen brown boxes stacked on shelves and a large refrigerator tucked into a corner with a lock on it. There was also a table and chair out back. There was a place for a computer but it had been ripped from the wall and likely used to crush the head of a Z. Chunks of it were scattered across the floor. I pulled down the boxes, a couple had some bars of soap, and a few others had Kraft Easy Mac Triple Cheese microwave cups.

I threw those to one side, they could come in handy.

Another box had twenty bottles of BBQ sauce. I opened one and squeezed some into my mouth. Yep, not something I would advise anyone doing but without any meat that was the closest I was getting to a T-bone. I coughed and spat the rest out. As I wiped the corner of my mouth I glanced at the refrigerator. It was white, with a silver handle. It kind of looked like the type that employees would use to stash their lunch in, except this sucker had a gleaming silver lock on the outside. Who the hell locked a refrigerator?

I scanned the room for anything I could use to break the lock off with. I went back out front and gazed around.

"You okay, bud?" Baja asked.

I didn't reply. I went over and grabbed the axe off

his back.

"Just borrowing this for a sec."

Back in the storage area I took a few sharp swings at the lock and it came off. I tossed the axe to one side and hesitated before opening. Maybe it was my imagination playing tricks on my mind or having seen one too many horror movies, but I was damn sure something was going to pop out.

"I'm pretty sure there's no zombie midget inside there."

I turned to find Jess leaning against the wall with her arms crossed, looking amused. I smirked before kicking the door handle and backed up. As it swung open I peered in and grimaced as a human head toppled out.

"I think I found the employee of the month."

On the ground in front of us was a severed head. The skull was caved in, and still had a piece of the computer monitor embedded in one eye. Now, had that been the only thing inside I might have been somewhat depressed. It wasn't. Above that on a separate shelf was a moldy sandwich and five cans of unopened Budweiser.

I swear, I got down on my knees and kissed the floor like it was hallowed ground.

“And you kiss me with those lips?” she said.

“Ah come on, you gotta admit, this is heavenly.” I scooped up the beers by the plastic ring. When we joined the others, Baja was on me faster than a whore on crack. I tossed a can to Dax, Izzy, and Specs and was in the process of taking a swig from my own when I looked at Garret. His eyes were open. He wasn’t looking any better but he had a slight curl to his lip. I walked over to him.

“Here, dude, I think you deserve some.”

I brought the beer can up to his lips.

He gulped some down but then coughed most of it out.

“Sorry, I’m gonna miss this.”

“Nah, you’re gonna make it. Hang in there, man,” I said.

He stifled a laugh.

“Look, um.” I paused, dropping my chin. “I’m

sorry about going off on you back at the library."

"No apologies needed."

I nodded slowly, appreciative.

"Johnny, bring me the comms unit."

I frowned. "You know how to work it?"

"They do teach us a few things in the secret society." He let out another chuckle that ended up being more cough than laughter. I scrambled over to it and dragged it back. Before I handed it to him I asked him a question. "Can these people be trusted?"

"Did I at any point attempt to harm you?" he replied.

I studied him. Even if he were lying I probably wouldn't have picked up on it.

"Tell me and be honest. You knew there wasn't a cure at the CDC, didn't you? That's where you were when this thing kicked off. You went for this unit and those men were yours?"

He blinked hard, and tried to lean forward. Kat and I helped him.

"In the event that I lost contact with the president, my orders were to get his daughter to safety. This is the only way to reach NORAD."

"Let me guess, the telephone number is 1-800-NORAD?" Baja said, strolling over swigging his beer like a boss. Garret smirked. I think even he was warming up to him. Which said a lot.

"That's not your run-of-the-mill military comms unit though, is it?" Dax asked.

"And you would know?"

"Did four years in the Marines. I never saw anything like that."

"It's not rocket science, it's easy to carry, lightweight, and does the job," he replied.

It wasn't a bulky unit. It couldn't have been bigger than a tablet computer. Except it had a wireless earpiece that Garret jammed into his ear.

"If the power is out, how the hell's that gonna work?" Dax asked.

"You want me to give you a technology lesson, or

do you want to get the hell out of here?"

As Garret began fiddling with the device, it flashed on. The UI had the seal of the President of the United States. Garret tapped in what appeared to be a password.

Baja leaned closer. Garret looked up at him and Baja backed up.

"I knew it. I told you that's some serious Area 51 shit. From the moment I laid eyes on it. Garret, before you die, is it true? Do we have downed UFOs from other planets?"

I tossed my empty can of Budweiser at him. "Dude."

"What?" he replied as if he couldn't see how utterly ridiculous he was acting.

"NORAD, this is Eagle One, come in." Garret repeated himself three times. We watched curiously as they must have requested a code. It was numerical.

"6198320443888."

How well did we know our government? So much of what they did was shrouded in secrecy. But with secrets came the need to lie. How long had they been lying about their use of biological weapons? What other weapons had they deployed that had been the cause of wars? I was all for protecting our country but to what extent?

Garret's conversation didn't last long. Most of it was short sound bites.

"That's a negative," Garret said. "Overrun. Yep."

He nodded.

"Roger that."

When the call ended he removed the earpiece.

"Twelve hours. There'll be choppers at Salt Lake City Airport."

I glanced at my watch; it was three thirty in the afternoon. That meant we would have to be there no later than three in the morning.

"Wouldn't they use Hill Air Force Base?" Kat asked.

"It's overrun. Plus it's too far out of the city. The airport is only ten minutes from here."

"Let's move," I said.

We tried to lift Garret up but he groaned in agony.

"Leave me here."

"We're not doing that," Kat said.

"I'm not going to make it. It's already begun."

He coughed again hard.

"Then I'll stay with you."

"Don't be stupid, go with them. Get on that chopper."

"No. You didn't leave me alone. I'm not leaving you here to die by yourself."

Garret stared at her before glancing at us.

"It's okay, we'll stay for a while, you know, until…" I said.

* * *

A spark of hope could be felt among us as darkness fell. Hours from now, in the early hours of the morning under the cover of night, we would slip out and make a dash for the Salt Lake City Airport. Choppers would be waiting to pick us up.

I was certain all of us were thinking about the same

thing. What was it going to be like to be under the protection of the U.S. government? How bad could it be? If anyone was prepared to survive the worst, it was all the fat cats at the top. If Specs's father had one hell of a supply in his underground shelter, how much more did the government? They had prime real estate, the best money could buy, and protection behind 25-ton blast doors in a granite mountain.

Kat sat with Garret for as long she could until he began to show signs that he was slipping away. Even then she held his hand muttering words we couldn't hear. How strange it must have been to live out your life being followed by the Secret Service day in and day out. Having them watching over you as personal bodyguards. Ready at any moment to take a bullet or whisk you away to a safe location.

I thought about those we had met in our short time in the city. Benjamin Garcia and Elijah. Both were from opposite sides of the tracks and yet they still helped us. Neither of them wanted to leave. I was sure Benjamin would. How could one person cope under this strain alone? I looked at Baja, Specs, Izzy, Jess, and Dax and now Ralphie. As much as we got on each other's nerves, we were family. A unit that moved together watching each other's backs. And in what remained of society that meant everything. I was certain if we weren't together, I would have lost my mind weeks ago.

Elijah, well, that was different. He was like us in many ways, tied to a group through association. Blood or not. Loyalty ran strong through any group that had been together a long time. The thought of staying in the city didn't sit well with me. Could we have found a place to hunker down like Benjamin? Found enough resources in apartments, stores, and factories? Possibly. But what would it matter? Eventually we would run out of food, water, and ammo. Then what would we become? Animals?

We needed hope, we needed something to drive us to a better tomorrow. Even if it was built upon lies. Governed by rulers who had no clue what they were doing. Maybe they did? Maybe they were like us, just looking out for their own interests. Trying to protect the ones they loved at all costs. That I could I understand.

I watched as thirty Z's shuffled their way through the gas station. They moved with purpose in the same direction. What had they heard or seen? Were others like us moving through the city searching for some glimmer of hope? Trying to escape the dead? Searching for people who might offer them care or comfort, or simply just food and water? How many had survived or knew what had caused this horrific outbreak?

Thousands in the city died in a matter of weeks, and that was just Salt Lake. The thought that this had hit all over the United States and most possibly the world was daunting. It was enough to break anyone.

Society had shot backwards in a matter of weeks. Some would never fathom how quickly a human could succumb to what they may have kept at bay inside of them. Now the streets were full of those who would shoot you without batting an eye, just for a meal. Others who would rape you, not because they were drunk or on drugs, but simply because they could get away with it. Of course there would be those out there that thought life would be just be a bed of roses. Folks who were naïve to think that everything would continue as normal. That human decency would triumph over evil. I wanted to believe that as much as anyone else, but when I thought about all we had seen, all I could think was...

Wake up and smell the coffee!

Nothing was the same now. It never would be.

How much had we relied on our creature comforts, expecting them always to be there?

They were gone and so were our loved ones. It wasn't what I saw outside that frightened me, it was what I didn't see inside me that did. What I might become if pushed too far?

"We're getting out of this, brother. This is it," Dax said as he tossed peanut shells into a can in front of him.

I glanced at him. "I hope so. I really do."

STANDOFF

Seven hours, and we would be on our way to the last defense against a world that had gone to the shitter and forgot to wipe its ass. It seemed a little too good to be true to think that we were going to get out of this mess. The hours had passed fast since Garret delivered the news. Now all there was left to do was wait.

But that was our mistake.

It was around eight in the evening when we knew were in trouble. Lights from approaching vehicles circulating the block for the past hour cast shadows on the walls. We assumed it was either the Grim Reapers doing their rounds, or other survivors. What we didn't realize was we had been spotted earlier that day. Why they had waited until now was anyone's guess. Perhaps they were assessing the situation, seeing if we were with another gang or group?

Specs flicked on a flashlight to check his ammo.

"Turn that off," Dax snapped.

"I need to see."

Dax snatched it out of his hand and flipped the switch.

"Sorry," Specs replied, realizing what he'd done.

Dax, Baja, and I had crawled up to the front window of the store and peered out behind a life-size cutout of a big pink Energizer Bunny that had been inserted into the window to promote a new kind of rechargeable battery. Had there been daylight, it would have looked as if it was giving birth to Baja. He was sneaking a peek between its legs every minute to see if they were approaching.

"What have you got?" Dax asked.

"A box of shells," I said while the others reeled off what they had for ammo. We had burned through a lot since leaving Benjamin's place. There was more than enough to get us over to the airport and hold off a small group of Z's but not for a standoff with a gang.

"You think they know we're in here?" Ralphie asked.

Dax squinted, nodding. "That armored truck hasn't moved for the past twenty minutes." They had pulled up right outside the gas station. Two of them, dressed in black with cream khakis, and blue bandanas, popped out of the back. They were talking among themselves. One of them lit a cigarette and cast a glance behind him.

"Maybe they need gas?" Specs asked.

"Nah."

I looked back at Jess and Izzy. They had been watching the back entrance. There were no windows out back, but at least if anyone tried to bust in the door they would end up riddled with bullets, and an arrow in their dick. Only the past hour had we managed to pry Kat away from Garret. He'd stopped breathing. It was only a matter of time before his eyes would open, the jaw would move, and he'd be looking for his first meal. We stayed low to the ground moving around. There was no telling if and when they were going to move in on us. Just that they were keeping watch. I didn't wait for Garret to turn, once Kat was out of sight I drove my knife into the back of his skull, twisted and pulled back out, using his shirt to clean it.

"What do you think they are waiting for?" Ralphie asked.

Just as he said that the inside of the shop was flooded with light, then it fell into darkness as another vehicle pulled alongside the armored truck. It was a green military jeep. I kind of figured they would have alerted others to our presence. There was no way I was going to die from a bullet of a gangbanger.

"Back up," Dax said cautiously to Ralphie who was getting a little too close to him for comfort. There were even more of them, six jumped out, each one carrying an assault rifle. They paused for a few seconds talking among themselves before looking our way.

Maybe Dax caught something I didn't but he began moving back.

"Get back from the windows."

"What?" Ralphie asked.

"Get back—"

I'd never seen Dax move so fast. Bullets snapped over our heads and glass shattered on top of us. Fragments flew through the air cutting us. Ralphie let go of his gun and instantly curled into a fetal position, clinging to his ears. I dropped flat on my face with glass hitting me from every angle. The noise was deafening. The pain was a wake-up call.

Baja and Specs scurried around behind the counter, while Dax took cover behind one of the shelving aisles. It wasn't much use. Shit was flying everywhere; packets of dry noodles, tins of beans, magazines, and chunks of the wall. The whole shop became like a giant piñata and we felt like candy stuck inside just waiting to drop.

As soon as they stopped to reload, we were up returning fire. I got lucky and hit one of them square in the chest, he fell back against the truck. Dax took out three of them with head shots. He always was the better shooter. Outside they were shouting in Spanish, and taking cover behind the truck and jeep. Bullets were ricocheting off the metal. More lights washed in. We could hear them yelling to one another. About what? Fuck knows!

"Why don't we aim for the gas pump?" Izzy shouted

"This is not the bloody movies, Izzy. It's going to take more than a bullet to blow this place. And then what? For all we know the gas tanks might be directly below us. Any more bright ideas?"

She didn't take kindly to his remarks. If he had already pissed her off, he was now definitely off her Christmas card list.

Then, for a moment there was silence. We took the moment to catch a breath only to find ourselves scrambling when Baja spotted one of them lining up with an RPG. These bitches were not messing around. It was the closest we had come to war, and it was happening right now in a fucking 7-Eleven of all places.

"Holy crap!" he hollered.

After the explosion of the RPG tearing its way through the store, and reducing a quarter of the store to open sky, we were pissed, but not as much as Baja.

"You gangbanging motherfuckers." Baja stood straight up and began unloading round after round at them in one continual spray like a scene from a Rambo movie.

"Get down," Dax screamed but Baja wasn't paying any attention. Thankfully Specs was, he reached up and dragged Baja down to the ground by the back of his pants, causing his naked ass to become exposed to Jess, Izzy, and Kat.

"Shit, dude. Are you trying to get yourself killed?" Dax hollered.

"Nice ass," Izzy joked. Baja flipped her the bird. It was good to see they hadn't lost their sense of humor in the middle of what was pure chaos. Then again I'd heard of cops and military folk doing the same thing in the field. It was something to do with the trauma of witnessing horror after horror. It wasn't that you lost sight of what you were in, it was just you needed something to keep yourself from losing it.

"Dax," I yelled through the noise of gunfire. "We need to get out of here now. There's no way we are going to match them shot for shot. There's more of them than us and probably even more on the way."

"You think?" he spat back.

Ralphie yelled from his fetal position. "Why the hell are they doing this?"

Baja popped out from behind the counter, covered in dust, looking like a soldier from Afghanistan.

"I don't know, maybe they want to cash their Lotto ticket," Baja added, grinning. Specs jabbed him in the gut with the butt of his gun as he scrambled over to where we were.

More glass came crashing down on top of Ralphie. "Fuck," Ralphie replied.

"Ralphie, get your gun and get your ass over here now."

He shook his head. The poor guy was paralyzed by fear. All of us were either crouched, laid flat, or had our backs up against anything that would provide cover. A few more shots unloaded, peppering the wall behind us. It was only a matter of time before they would start moving in.

That last round must have caused Izzy to break a nail or something as she started returning rapid fire like a mercenary who'd had enough of being in the jungle. Yeah, that girl knew how to put a guy in place. I pitied Dax. Maybe it was for the best.

I took advantage of the additional cover to slide my way across the floor like a bloody lizard heading for Ralphie. Once I reached him, I took a hold of the back of his belt and attempted to drag. I say attempt because it was nothing more than that. Now I knew he was a heavy fella from the moment I laid eyes on him, but I swear I felt like a five-year-old trying to drag a Mack truck with its brakes on.

"Dude, get your ass up," I screamed at him.

He shook his head. I was about to try again when a DVD hit me in the side of the head.

"What the fuck?"

I rubbed my head and looked down. It was a workout DVD with some bitch from the '80s wearing a pink leotard. Of course Baja thought this was fucking hilarious. His timing was so off I felt like shooting him in the leg right there and then just to snap him out of it.

"Dude, your constant marijuana usage has dulled what remaining brain cells you have."

Fortunately, I didn't have to struggle for much longer, Specs joined me and we hauled Ralphie's fat ass behind cover. I took a hold of his handgun and wrapped his mitts around it.

"This fear. Swallow it now or it's going to get you killed. Now fight or sit there like a coward and watch us die."

Yeah, okay, maybe I was being a little hard on him but with live bullets firing at us every two seconds and those fuckers outside using an RPG on us, this wasn't a time for wimping out. But how many times had that happened to soldiers on the front line? They froze up and couldn't think? They rolled over and wished they had taken that shitty job at Walmart instead.

I scoffed thinking of all the asinine ads on TV that the military used to lure in kids no older than me. How the military tried to portray the career as being badass. Jumping out of airplanes, gliding out of water all stealth and shit, only to take down the enemy in between munching down a cheese sandwich.

It was bullshit. Oh no, but you rarely heard the stories from those whose buddies shit their pants and cried for their mothers. No, those were buried under a mat along with the other political fuckups that no one would ever hear. All America wanted to hear about were the heroes. Give us the heroes! The guy who took out a hundred ragheads with one bullet, or survived a landmine and got up with a leg dangling off and soldiered on like a boss. They wanted someone they could pin a Purple Heart on. Someone who could appear on *Good Morning*

America and would say it was an honor to bleed for the red, white, and blue. Please! What a crock of crap. The truth was no one knew how they were going to react until they were out there. No amount of infomercials about being the best you could be, was going to help you man up when the shit hit the fan.

Real war wasn't like Rambo, it was more like a street fight without gloves. There were no rules; no easy way through it and it could turn deadly in a heartbeat.

Shit! I was beginning to sound like my old man. I scoffed thinking about him. Man, he would have loved this. Dax looked over at me with a look of despair.

"About getting out of this," Dax started to say.

"No you don't, we're getting out," I shot back. Right then in that moment I did something I never imagined I would do, I took a hold of his head and pressed it against mine the way our father would.

"Hoorah!" I said. I didn't say it as loud as they did but loud enough to make him snap out of his spiral down into pity party for one please.

Dax looked right back in my eyes. I'm sure he couldn't believe it himself. His lip curled up. Then like getting an adrenaline shot to his system, his eyes widened.

"Hoo fuckin' rah!" And just like that he was back in the game. "Now listen up you pussies, we're going to lay down some serious heat, while the rest of you slip out the back."

"Dax, they'll have it covered," Jess replied.

"So? We either shoot our way out of here, or they're coming in. Either way there's a chance we're dead. So make a choice."

She gritted her teeth and nodded affirmatively. It was hard to think when all around us gunfire was erupting furiously. Through the shelving I could see them getting closer. Two of them had crept up past the gas pumps. I noticed they had something in their hands.

"Flashbang," I yelled before hitting the ground.

The others followed suit. My eyes squeezed shut saving me from the flash of blinding light, but not the ringing in my ears. I didn't wait for them to push forward. I shoved the barrel of my Benelli SuperNova Tactical Pump through the shelving unit and unleashed my load. Baja and Specs took out the two guys who had tossed the flashbang and were trying to retreat like little bitches. I glanced to my side, thinking Ralphie would be curled up in a ball. Instead, he was up, gun in hand and unloading rounds at them.

"Go," Dax yelled. I gestured to Baja and Specs to move with Jess, Izzy, and Kat while we continued to rain a torrent of bullets down on them. There was no time to see if they had made it out or even survived. We were in a constant state of battle. I heard gunfire ring out from behind but that was it.

What happened next occurred fast.

Three Molotov cocktails shot past us. They must have come up the sides and moved in. The wall behind and floor in front of us exploded in fire and within a matter of minutes the place was engulfed in tongues of fire. Thick black smoke smothered the air. Coughing and choking we crawled our way back into the rear storage area. We had no time to check who was outside or what we were running into.

Our lungs were gasping for air.

All I heard was the sound of guns cocking as I hit the floor on my knees. My eyes were burning, snot was coming out of my nose. I looked up for a second and found a cold hard barrel of steel pressed against my face. I shot a sideways glance and saw the others on their knees surrounded by at least forty men.

I glanced at my watch. We had six hours until pickup.

TEMPLE SQUARE

What's it like being captured by the enemy in wartime? I'm not sure, but I can tell you it must have been a hell of lot better than being snagged by these little gangbanging bitches. I would have given anything to find a volume dial. Their incessant jeering was grinding my hump. I expected their leader Domino to show up but he didn't. If it hadn't been for one of them I was certain they would have killed us right there and then, execution style.

One of them bounced back and forward. "I say we drop these bitches, homie."

"You heard what Domino said."

"Fuck what he says, they killed our brothers."

"I know, little man, and they'll pay."

I tried to look up but one of them pistol-whipped me. I felt warm blood trickle down the side of my face.

Droplets hit the floor in front of me. I glanced to my right expecting to see Baja, Specs, and the others but neither of them were there. Jess, Izzy, and Kat were present but not them. Had they killed them?

"Throw them in the truck and take 'em back."

"I'm telling you this is wrong. I say we do them here. Domino won't know."

One of them brought his gun up underneath the chin of the other. "Do I have to tell you again?"

The other sneered in contempt. "Fernando, Pablo, Emilio."

Three younger guys hustled over and yanked us up. They strong-armed us to the back of an armored truck. We were all thrown in together. They didn't bother tying us, as we didn't stand a chance with or without restraints. They slammed the metal doors shut. We were instantly engulfed in darkness.

"You okay?" I asked Jess.

"Yeah."

"What happened to Baja and Specs?"

"I don't know. It all happened fast. They were there one minute and gone the next."

"Did they shoot them?"

"Gunfire erupted when we got out the back. It's possible."

I let out a heavy sigh. The thought of them dead weighed heavy on my mind.

The truck bumped its way down the road. Outside we could hear the occasional sound of gunfire as they shot at Z's. A few times we jerked back and forward. No doubt they were plowing their way through the dead on their way to Temple Square. Beyond that it was silent in the truck. I don't think any of us planned for this, or knew what to expect. But I was sure that each of us felt that we weren't going to come out of this unscathed.

The truck jerked to a stop. The sound of boots, then the door unlocked.

"C'mon, get out."

They didn't wait for us, they pulled at us like dogs on a leash. The first thing I saw set the tone for the entire place. Stripped naked, impaled on a post that was only illuminated by small fires around it was the president of the United States. I turned, wanting to block Kat from seeing it but was beaten forward with the butt of a gun. The sound of her cries behind me would be something I would never forget. I made it a few steps before casting a glance over my shoulder. Kat had collapsed.

"Get up, bitch."

"Leave her alone." Jess pushed back against them and was backhanded. Izzy saw red and lunged at the guy. That's when they realized they should have restrained us. I pushed through two of them. I didn't care in that moment if they put a bullet in my head. All I wanted to do was tear a limb off the guy that touched Jess. I don't think they realized the full extent of who they were fucking with. Right there fists flew. I right-hooked a guy and knocked him to the ground. Dax turned and grabbed another by the neck. I lunged at one more only to find my legs taken out from underneath me. They began pummeling us with the butts of their assault rifles. Pain shot through me as one hit me in the back of the head.

Then a gun went off. I thought for a split second they had shot one of us.

"Enough."

Instantly, the beating stopped.

With blood streaming down my forehead, and one eye swollen, I looked up to see a man in a dark navy suit, white shirt, red tie, and shiny black shoes heading towards us. I blinked hard. He held a handgun down by his side.

"This isn't how we treat out guests."

Guests? What fucking planet was this guy from?

He looked the complete opposite of the others. Older, clean-cut, and in full control of them. *Domino,* I thought.

I wasn't sure what to expect. I imagined he would be covered in tattoos, sporting a mouthful of gold, and wearing the same ragtag bargain bin clothing like the others. Instead he looked as if he had walked in from another dimension. A world untouched by the brutality, loss, and scarcity. The kind that permeated and smothered us like a film of dirt every day.

"I'm sorry for the way you have been treated."

"I bet you are," I spat blood near his foot, glancing up at the body of the president. He followed my eyes.

"Ah, yes, him." He breathed in deeply, admiring his sick handiwork. "It seemed appropriate. A..." he paused searching for the words, "living statue, well, a dead one. But perfect, wouldn't you agree?"

Kat leapt up, spitting at him, her hands clawing the air. She didn't make it even a few feet before a couple of his men took a hold of her. Domino looked at her like a lost kitten. Was it pity he felt, or did he feel anything? He tilted his head to one side and ran his hand down the side of her cheek, collecting her tears. Kat flinched at his touch.

"Bring them up. I'm sure they haven't eaten."

It was the most peculiar encounter I'd had with someone who was meant to strike fear in the hearts of those who double-crossed him. Yet what I saw before me was an anomaly to what I had pictured in my mind.

His men pulled me to my feet and dragged me forward. As he led us through the grounds he began pointing out different landmarks as if he was a tour guide, or the owner of it all. Yet, that's what he was. He had claimed a substantial portion of the city, including sections that were steeped in history and had at one time attracted droves of visitors from around the world.

"We have a history and art museum over there, the Joseph Smith Memorial Building. You are absolutely going to love what I have in store for you there." He continued gazing at everything as if he was seeing it for the first time too. "Back there we have the temple and the tabernacle."

We ambled behind in utter bewilderment. Was this guy for real? We followed him into a large white building. A sign outside read the Joseph Smith Memorial Building. Inside was a multi-story lobby with marble floors and pillars, cathedral-high ceilings. In its time it must have been a masterpiece. No expense had been wasted. An expensive chandelier lay in pieces on the ground, blood smeared pillars, steps, and walls. If the walls could speak, what horrors would they have witnessed here? Had people fallen prey to walkers, or his men?

We passed two of his guys who were in the process of cleaning with rags. The water inside the bucket was stained red.

"Forgive the décor, we are renovating," Domino muttered.

It felt like I was having an out-of-body experience. It was surreal. We were led up ten flights of steps. On every floor we listened to a running commentary coming from Domino's mouth. By the time we made it to what was called the Roof Restaurant I was more than convinced that he was insane. He honestly believed that the outbreak was meant to happen.

It was destiny, he said.

A changing of power from one ruler to another was all part of nature's way of bringing balance back to a world off kilter. In his mind, that's why the president was there when all hell broke loose. He took narcissism to a whole new level by pointing out areas where he said his portrait would be hung. In time a statue would be made in his likeness. The entire temple and any worship that would occur would be dedicated to him. All I could think about was how good it would feel to shove a knife right through his smug face. That was going to be my offering.

Everywhere, carpet was soaked in blood. We entered a circular room with a large dome above us. It was made from stained glass. A double set of dark wooden doors brought us into a two-tier dining area. At one time it would have had a breathtaking view of Temple Square and the downtown of Salt Lake City. At night it would have been lit up but now all you could see was a city thrown into darkness. Fire burned in areas of the city. The whole view screamed hopeless. It was a stark reminder of our reality.

"By the way, I haven't introduced myself."

"Domino, we already know," I said.

"I see my reputation precedes me."

"Yeah, and not in a good way. More like… Jeffery

Dahmer."

Domino's smile dropped.

"Don't mistake my hospitality for weakness."

He gestured to a few men. They nodded and disappeared. We were guided into a semi-circle booth that was made of green leather. The edges were formed from a deep red wood. Fifteen men watched over us as we sat at a table covered in a pristine white tablecloth. The cutlery was clean enough you could see your face in it. The whole place had a creepy feel to it as if someone had just upped and abandoned it in a hurry. Plates, cutlery, and wine glasses were still laid out on every single table in the restaurant.

His men returned within a matter of minutes with a metal trolley covered in all manner of food. It wasn't restaurant food but it was real, hot, and something we hadn't seen in a while. Chicken, fries, sausages, peas, beans, and rolls of bread. Where had they got this from?

"Eat up."

Kat sat there unable to. We also hesitated, unsure of

what was going on. Yes, we had food in front of us but we had killed his men. Weren't we his enemy?"

"Come, eat." He gestured to the bowls of steaming hot food.

We continued scanning it and looking at him until he banged his hand on the table so hard the whole thing shook violently.

"Fucking eat," he screamed. And there it was, the side that we had heard of hidden below a mask he wanted to portray. He honestly thought he was a good man. That somehow nature was working together for him to be commander-in-chief.

I slowly put a roll to my lips and sniffed it. Was he planning on poisoning us? Cautiously we each took a bite and then another. As much as we had been affected by what we had seen outside, hunger overrode anything we were feeling. We devoured what was in front of us within a matter of five minutes. Four bottles of wine were brought out and opened. It was strange being served by a gangbanger with a white cloth draped over his inked arm.

Meanwhile, the rest of Domino's men watched on with a finger loosely on the trigger.

"Are you going to tell us why you've brought us in?" I asked.

"I thought you might be able to shed some light on what our good president was muttering about before he took his final breath," Domino replied.

Kat dropped her fork. Her hands were shaking. Jess reached to comfort her.

"Stop it," Domino shouted at her.

"But."

"She's grieving, can't you see?"

Now this was odd on a level far beyond I had ever seen, he acknowledged Kat's grief and yet he didn't want Jess to comfort her. He had murdered her father, the president of the United States, and now he was telling someone else what not do when the tears were caused by him.

"But—"

He banged his fork down against his plate. "Leave

her alone. You are not helping."

Was he posing the question to Jess or all of us?

Jess slowly pulled back and continued to eat as Kat sobbed helplessly.

"You see, that's the problem. We all want to solve each other's problems instead of just allowing them to be. How can we change, grow, become strong if we keep trying to rule over others' emotions?"

"I was just trying to comfort her," Jess muttered.

"No. You were uncomfortable with her tears. You don't care about her. You only care about how you feel."

He closed his eyes and breathed deeply. It was odd behavior.

"What did the president say?" I asked, changing the subject.

His eyelids popped open and he continued eating as though nothing had taken place. "Something about a cure?"

I shook my head. "No, doesn't ring a bell."

He eyed me across the table, then looked at Dax

and Ralphie.

"What's your name?" he asked.

"Me?"

He nodded.

"Johnny."

"Well, Johnny, I don't believe you."

He picked at his teeth with a butter knife.

"You see, when I found our..." he chuckled, "commander-in-chief, after a good amount of... what shall I say, coaxing, he was more than willing to tell me that the CDC had discovered a cure. In fact, he begged me to spare his life."

He told them?

His eyes went to Kat. "He spoke of you. Do wish to know what he said?"

She stared at him.

"He wanted you to know how much he loved you, and that if I was to ever find you, that I would promise not to harm you. Of course I'm a fair man. But, I'm a businessman. Nothing's changed that. No amount of the dead walking the streets has changed that. I gave him an option. Tell me where the cure was. He offered me nothing, so I took the only thing he had to give." He paused. "His life."

His eyes drifted back to me.

"Now tell me what you know."

"Like I said, we don't—"

Before I could say another word he slammed his knife down into Kat's hand so hard it went through and stood upright in the table. She let out a bloodcurdling scream. Dax jumped up but before he could do anything, the men had their weapons on him.

"You bastard." I rose to my feet. Two of his men gripped my shoulders, figuring I was going to lunge at him.

"By the time we are done here, you will tell me what I want to know," he said.

"No, by the time I'm done, you will be dead," I replied. Our eyes were fixed on each other's. I don't think either of us blinked. It was like seeing the reflection of the devil himself. Pure evil masquerading as light.

FIGHT OR DIE

The first thing Domino did when we refused to give him the answers he wanted was to have his men take us into one of the twelve banquet rooms in the building. I kind of figured it was only temporary. No doubt his plans with us involved pain.

They forcefully shoved us inside and locked the doors behind us. In a weird twist of fate, the room we had been placed inside was called the President's Room, located on the ninth floor. There were three large arched windows, a white pillar in the center of the room, and the walls were painted in jade, country-blue, and beige colors.

But it wasn't anything related to the real president. Displayed on the walls were portraits of fifteen presidents of the Church of the Latter-day Saints.

"Ok, this is freaky," Ralphie said, strolling around.

"Is it me or do they look like they are eyeballing us?" He ambled over to one. "Don't you go eyeballing me, boy," he said in a Southern accent, "or I'll give you fifty lashings of the birch."

"Who does their décor? This is nasty," Izzy spat.

Dax and I went to the far end and tugged on the windows but they were locked. The only furniture inside the spacious square room was an upright, dark wood piano with a stool and a podium. I immediately snatched up the stool.

"Stand back."

I tossed it as hard as I could at the window then turned away, expecting glass to go everywhere. Instead it just bounced off not even leaving a scratch.

"Are you shitting me?"

"Out of the way, wimp," Dax said, picking it up and sticking out his chest. He hurled it. The window cracked ever so slightly. He scooped it up again and repeated the same thing three times before he went a deep shade of red and gave up. Were they expecting their windows to be shot at? The glass was as tough as diamond.

Ralphie went over to the piano and began playing his rendition of "Chopsticks," and then broke into playing some made-up song with the lyrics, *We are so fucked.* The longer he played the more violent he started to become with the keys until he stepped back and kicked the piano with his heel. White and black keys flew off in every direction.

"Whoa! Steady on, Jerry Lee Lewis," I said coming over to him and gripping the back of his collar. The two of us just stared at the now destroyed piano. It was hard to get a grip on our emotions. They were all over the place. Jess had torn a piece of her own shirt off and wrapped it around Kat's swollen and bloody hand. I could barely comprehend what Domino had done to her, let alone her father.

Inside that room, three hours passed. Every ten minutes a couple of men would check in on us. We sat, we wandered, and at times took out our frustration by destroying anything in the room that wasn't held down. I wondered what was going through each of their minds, but more importantly what had happened to Baja and Specs. It was after midnight, three hours until the choppers would arrive. I leaned my forehead against the pane of glass and peered down. They used rod-shaped wood with rags on the end to create makeshift torches. The flames licked the air. Some gang members stood watch, while others had turned over boxes and were playing what looked like a game of craps. In the distance beyond the temple I could see the inside of a building lit up. I closed my eyes, allowing my mind to drift into the past.

"Johnny, now remember, squeeze the trigger slowly. Breath out as you apply pressure."

"Like this?"

"That's it, son. Remember equal height, equal light."

My father was referring to centering the front sight air gaps with the left and right dots on the rear of the handgun. Once that was done you lined up the front and rear sights for equal height.

It was the key to aiming straight.

A sudden noise and I squinted to see how I had done. He had been showing me how to shoot for the first time. Everything could affect your aim from the size of the grip, to how you cradled it. Just a small amount of pressure from the hand that didn't have a finger on the trigger could send everything off kilter.

Initially I missed anything I fired at but over time my accuracy got better, and with it came a quiet confidence. Even then it was just the beginning. Next was shooting from behind an object, then moving and shooting. Repetition was the key, my father would say. Do it again. Do it again. It became ingrained in me. I could hear his voice even now as clear as day.

"One day, you might find yourself having to kill another man, Johnny. That gun has to become part of you. There are only three reasons you'll get shot. One, you're not paying attention. Two, you're uncomfortable handling a gun. Three, you can't shoot for shit."

I nodded, thinking my father walked on water.

After our mother died, he would make us sleep with a handgun. It was never loaded. But he wanted it to become second nature to us. Our father was strange that way. How many other kids at the age of eleven went to bed with a Glock 17?

Lost in my thoughts, I was snapped back into the present moment when the door burst open. Four of Domino's men came in. Two of them holding fiery torches, the others assault rifles, sweeping the room yelling my name. At first I couldn't make out what else they were saying as the main guy was speaking in Spanish. Frustrated that I wasn't following their directions, they came over and grasped me firmly by the arm and dragged me forward. Dax tried to intervene but one of the men aimed his handgun at his head. The others watched helplessly as they led me out of the room. I was the only one they took. As I crossed the threshold I made note of how many were outside. Two. I shot Dax a look and dropped my eyes to my fingers where I was signaling two. I had no idea where they were taking me. Why they had selected me, or if I would see the others again. For all I knew he was going to impale me alongside the president.

I was never religious. I had my father to thank or perhaps blame for that. But in that moment I swear I said a prayer. It was nothing much. Just a few words murmured under my breath. *If you're real, I could really use your help now.* I don't know what I was expecting? An angel, a flash of light, or Ashton Kutcher to jump out and tell me I had just been punk'd, but nothing happened. At least, that's what I thought.

They brought me down to ground level and ushered me out into the night air where they met with two more men. I glanced at my watch. It was close to one in the morning. Two more hours. That's all we had left. What the hell were they doing up at this time of night? I could hear a crowd in the distance, rap music blaring and the steady pulsating of a bass. I cast a look upward towards the room they had us in. The windows were dark. If Dax and the others were watching, I couldn't see them.

Pushed forward, I stumbled. That only infuriated them more. One cursed and batted me in the back with the butt of his gun. We were heading towards Salt Lake Tabernacle. It was a huge dome-shaped auditorium. The roof was a shiny aluminum resting on top of a sandstone foundation. Fire flickered, casting shadows against the walls and ground as I was pushed through the doorway. It was like entering an MMA event. Gangbangers were jeering, shouting, and even tossing empty beer cans in my direction. Someone spat at me. Others took advantage of the moment to land a few blows. Whatever I was being led into, it wasn't good. The noise of the crowd grew louder, their voices echoing off the roof above. Above the bobbing heads I saw a steel cage octagon. I glanced up to the second tier above us. More men filled out the space and were tossing down toilet paper rolls that unraveled as they hit their targets below. The smell of weed lingered in the air as I found myself outside the cage. Domino was seated and talking to a good-looking girl in her twenties. She was wearing a tight shiny outfit that reminded me of the seventies.

"Ah, glad you could join us." He rose to his feet and clasped the sides of my shoulders. "You are just in time for the main attraction."

"Which is?" I asked inquisitively.

"You of course." He let out a deep rumble of laughter. I got a whiff of his bad breath and felt like gagging. He smelled like he'd swallowed a Z's ball sack.

"Isn't this a little past your bedtime?" I asked.

He sneered before breaking into a grin. "I like you. That's why I'm giving you a second chance to tell me what you know."

"What makes you think I know anything?"

He scanned the crowd. "Have you wondered why these men follow me?"

"Let me guess. You give good head?"

He scowled, and prodded his finger against my chest.

"You're a bit of smart ass. Now let's see if there's more to you than words."

I sighed growing weary of his drivel. "Is this where you kill me?"

He snorted. "I'm not going to kill you." He turned me by my shoulders. "He is."

Inside the steel cage was a beast of a man. He had to have been twice my height and three times as wide. He literally looked as if he had swallowed another human being. Bald, his entire face and upper half of his chest was tattooed. Numbers, spider webs, dots, tears, skulls, and all manner of explicit imagery. His earlobes hung like an African Zulu warrior, with two bones piercing them. He had muscle on top of muscle. Hell, he looked as if he lived beneath a bench press. He grinned, showing nothing but a gold grill.

They shoved me towards the steps that led up to a thick metal gate. One of the gang who was hanging off the side like a monkey reached down and unlocked it. Entering the cage, I looked back when I heard it lock. I gulped. My eyes immediately began looking for a way out, or at least a way to stay out of the reach of Arnold Schwarzenegger's Hispanic cousin.

The crowds roared a name. *Bones.* They repeated it over and over again. I was pretty sure it wasn't my nickname, and he wasn't called that because he had two in his ears. No, I didn't think it could get any worse than going hand to hand with Goliath. But it did. Tossed over the top of the cage, two medieval-looking weapons landed in the center of the octagon.

One was a one-handed flail. A sickening device that had a wooden handle with a chain attached to one end, and a spiked ball on the other. I'd seen these on Halloween in Castle Rock. But this was no kiddie replica. It was a real ball cracker. The other? A shitty little knife that might have been good for peeling a tomato, and that was it.

Bones didn't wait for me to decide how I wanted to be killed, he immediately went for the flail. He was fast, but then again I wasn't planning on getting my noggin cracked with that shit. I lunged forward as he bent down to pick it up and kicked him in the side. Now I was pretty damn sure my boots were going to give him air. Instead, it was like kicking a wall. He didn't move a fucking inch, and yet I bounced back a foot.

When I reared my head back up, the look on his face said it all. It turned from a grin into a scowl. The next thing I knew I was running around that ring hoping to break the four-minute mile with a tiny little knife that probably wasn't sharp enough to cut my toenails with.

Every time he swung the spiked ball it would rip into the wooden floor and tear up splinters the size of stakes. Now clearly I was at a disadvantage both in size and weaponry, never mind the fierce mustache he was sporting. He could have won an award for that in Movember. Yep, November, the time of the year all the pricks in our town grew thick mustaches.

I ducked as he swung his meat-shredding ball sack with fury.

Now I'd seen enough Muhammad Ali video clips

over at Baja's house to know when to dance like a butterfly and sting like a bee. And I'd like to say there was a strategy to my mad River Dance moves that I was doing to avoid becoming torn to shreds but there wasn't. I was just hoping I could wear him out, or at least make him consider dance academy. Unfortunately, it wasn't working.

From the time that flail hit the ground and got stuck to the time he managed to pry it loose, I figured I had about three seconds.

Now I knew I wasn't going to be able to hack his head off with that penis-size blade even if the ladies like to say, it isn't the size of your tool that matters, but how you use it.

It was a lie then, and it was a lie now.

The ball of metal tore into the floor and I saw my opportunity. With his wrist down tugging at the handle I came down on his arm with a lethal kick that would had made Baja proud. The fucking guy was holding it so tight his arm crunched beneath me. I toppled to the ground and scrambled to get clear but he wasn't rushing. He was yelling in agony. The bone hadn't pierced his skin but I had clearly unhinged some part of the joint below the muscle.

As he was screaming all manner of obscenities I came over to the side of the cage right in front of Domino and spat at him.

"Who's the bitch now? Get in here. I will…" I saw his eyes flare with excitement and I knew that meant only one thing. I dived to my side just before my head was nearly caved in by the weapon from hell. The meathead had snatched up the flail in his other hand. I kept him on his toes as I bounced my way around that cage like a man on speed. I was panting hard. My heart felt like it was about to burst out of my chest. I could hear my pulse ringing in my ears.

Once again as the flail came down, I scooted around him and cut Bones on the back of his legs. *Shit! This tiny thing does work?* He screamed in agony and swung the spiked ball again like a lunatic.

When I attempted to repeat the same move that had unhinged his one arm, Bones caught my leg. He spun me like a feather with one hand. I'd never felt such strength in my life. I smashed into the side of the cage. The sharp metal cut the side of my face. Blood began to trickle down. Now maybe I got lucky, but he never did get that flail back out of the floor. It was stuck in there stronger than the sword in the stone. While that had worked in my favor, what happened next didn't. Bones slammed his foot down on my back. I swear it might as well have been a ten-ton rock. Pain shot through me. He grabbed me by my neck and slammed his other hand into my nuts and lifted me up as if I weighed nothing more than a buck. I gasped as he tossed me from one side of the ring to the other. I slammed into the cage. I tried to get up fast but the muscles in my leg wouldn't have it. I spat blood. The crowd was going wild. This was like an MMA fight except no one was getting paid, and they had certainly screwed up the weight class.

I did my best to haul myself up, but he was on me

fast. I reached for my knife but it was gone. I must have dropped it. This time he held me above his head and walked around the cage as if waiting to get the word to break my back on his knee. I was certain I was going to die, or at least be sucking shit through tubes until the next apocalypse.

Without a weapon I was shit out of luck. Flailing around above him, I was incapacitated.

This was it. I was about to become this guy's toothpick.

Then he yelled something I didn't expect.

"Enough!" he shouted. "This is over."

Was my hearing fucked up? Did this guy really say that? Or was this all part of Domino's sick mind game; one final sense that you were going to get out of it, and then the deathblow.

Bones lowered me down. He then picked up the knife on the ground, approached the side of the cage, and tossed it at Domino, it missed and hit the floor.

"You missed," Domino said with a smug grin on

his face.

"We're done," Bones replied.

"You are done when I say you are."

With blood blurring my vision, I glanced over trying to make sense of it.

"Now kill him."

"Do it yourself, I'm done," Bones replied.

Domino smiled at me, then looked back at Bones. He raised a handgun towards him.

"Fight or die."

Now it's hard to argue with a gun. This fight had just become even stranger. Why had this man given up beating me to a pulp? I was contemplating this when two new medieval weapons landed within a few inches of my face. This time one was a sword, and the other was a poleaxe. Being that I was closest, I reached for the sword. Despite being thoroughly confused as to why he didn't kill me when he could have, I wasn't going to take any chances.

The crowd tossed bottles and cans at the cage. Beer sloshed onto the floor making it even harder to run. Bones turned back toward me. I was already up but hesitant to attack.

"Sorry, kid, I've got no choice."

I furrowed a frown. He really didn't want to kill

me. There I was imagining he was one of Domino's henchmen, and it seemed he was being forced to fight. He was just another pawn in the game. Bones scooped the axe, he swished back and forward as if familiarizing himself with it.

"I'll try to make this painless."

"That's comforting," I replied.

And there we were again facing off against each other like gladiators in the Colosseum. Our weapons clashed together with such force that sparks ignited, and my entire hands shook with pain. I was sure this time that I wouldn't be given a free pass. Now maybe it was the prayer I sent up to the big guy upstairs or perhaps I was just meant to survive, but over the chants of the crowd a sound echoed. I kid you not; it was the General Lee Dixie horn from *The Dukes of Hazzard.* It was so utterly bizarre that even Bones stopped and the crowd turned. As they did two men rushed into the building shouting something.

Once my ears adjusted to what was being said, it

became clear.

"We are under attack."

You would have thought it was Black Friday shopping at Walmart, the crowd piled out the door in a heartbeat. The sound of music was quickly replaced by gunfire, and the one thing I hoped I wouldn't hear. The moans of the dead.

Now I would like to say that I killed that insane asshole who had thrown my ass in the ring, but I didn't. Bones did. Upon seeing the crowd disperse, and Domino distracted by the chaos, Bones brought back his arm and launched that battle axe through the air. It soared through the metal bars and landed right between Domino's shoulders. It was one hell of a shot.

"Good shot," I commended him, and for a brief moment he turned and smiled. Then the crack of a gun echoed. Bones grasped his neck and I knew instantly he'd been hit. I turned to see Domino hit the floor and take his last breath. Maybe it was because Bones hadn't killed me, or simply because he was no longer holding an axe in his hand but I scrambled over to him. He was coughing and choking on his own blood. The bullet had penetrated one side of his neck and come out the other.

"Why didn't you kill me?"

Through gritted teeth that were stained now in blood he spoke, "Get out, go now."

I knew he wasn't going to make it. I was torn by what this man had done, or by what he hadn't. As I ran to the gate with the sound of gunfire, it was locked. I yanked on it hard but it wouldn't budge. Now what you have to know about this cage was it went up high. The vertical bars were over eight feet high. At the top they turned in and had barbed wire around the edges. Even if I could have climbed up, I would have been cut to bits trying to make my way over the razor-sharp metal.

"Here," Bones's gruff voice called out. I swiveled around to see him getting up. "Get on my shoulders."

"What?"

"Do it."

I wasn't going to argue. I climbed up on top of him

like a steel climbing frame. Every inch of him was pure muscle. Once I was on top he stood up, stumbled forward a little but clung to my legs.

"Stand up," he bellowed staggering around as if he was drunk. The blood gushing from his neck had got worse. He wouldn't last long and there was no way in hell I was going to stay in there with him as a Z. God help the person who would open the cage after he turned.

Like a circus act I gripped his bald head for support and rose upright. He clung to my calves and moved back and forward. I had a feeling I was going to be impaled on the ends of the steel cage if he slipped. But standing on his six foot four frame, I removed my jacket and tossed it over the barbed wire.

"Ready."

"Ok, dude, what the fuck are you going to do?"

He coughed then let out a stifled laugh. "You ever seen a Scottish caber toss?"

Before I could reply with a yes or no, he launched me upward so hard I nearly tossed up the contents of my stomach. I landed hard over the top of the barbed wire. My hands clinging to the edges. The sockets ached in pain. Beneath me, I saw Bones drop to his knees. One hand on the floor, the other on the side of his neck. He stared at me and I think he wanted to say something, instead he just collapsed. As much as I wished I could have thanked him, he was gone. The ruckus outside had reached a feverish pitch. Z's were making their way into the tabernacle. I slid down the outside of the cage until my boots hit the floor. I double-timed it over to Domino, snatched up his handgun, and made a beeline for the door.

I fired three rounds into a bunch of snarling Z's that were coming at me. When I made it outside I could now see what was going on. The place was overrun with Z's. It was pure madness. Among the mass of dead bodies, and gang members running in every direction, a car was zipping around, its occupants yelling like lunatics while shooting. It wasn't the occupants that made me know who it was; it was the car they had chosen. It was a 1979

Country Squire station wagon and none other than Baja was driving it, while Specs and two other black guys in the back were shooting up the place. I had never felt as relieved to see them than I did in that moment. Behind them in a jeep and five armored trucks were the Dark Kings. The sound of the Dixie Lee horn went off again and I heard Baja shout out, "Hey, Johnny B. Goode!" He then launched into singing that damn Chuck Berry song again while continuing to take head shots at anything and everything. I swear he shot the head off a statute. He was nearly as good with a gun as he was with a pair of nunchucks.

I was about to go get the others when I felt a smack to the side of my head.

"Where the fuck do you think you're going?"

It was the same guy who had collected us from the store.

Oh you've got to be kidding me.

"Get up, motherfucker."

He kicked me twice in the stomach, the second

time I grabbed his leg and swept out the other one. He landed hard but not enough to stop him. This guy was a serious scrapper. He jumped right back up like a fucking jack-in-the-box and launched into a prizefighter assault. I returned fist for fist. At one point he began to choke me. I saw stars and darkness creeping in at the edge of my eyes. I knew if I didn't get this punk off fast, it was going to be lights out. I brought my knee up and smashed it into his nuts with all the force I could muster.

He dropped and groaned in agony. It gave me a few seconds to catch my breath.

What I didn't know was he had reached into the front of his pants and pulled out a .40 semi-automatic handgun.

"Let's go, homie," he spluttered. "Fight or die."

I had enough of fighting. Down on my hands and knees I spotted the Glock beneath me. I clasped it and spun over and emptied the magazine into his chest until he was no longer a threat.

"I'll go with die." I spat a big glob of blood onto

the concrete in front of me. I scrambled over to him and took the handgun and headed towards the Joseph Smith Memorial Building. That's when I spotted Elijah. Wearing a black bandana with a white skull on it, he looked every bit the gang member that I remembered. He was holding two handguns and walking forward with all the confidence of a man ready to die. A shot to his left, then right, then behind him. He was taking down the dead and the Grim Reapers like a boss.

"Elijah," I yelled. His eyes darted over to me for a brief moment. "I need a hand to get the others out."

He nodded, kicking a Z back, and rushed towards me, calling for a few more of his men to follow. Gone were those guarding the front entrance. One of them lay on the ground, his stomach pulled inside out, brain matter and gristle spread inside a puddle of blood.

Inside we ascended the steps while two of his men took out Grim Reapers who'd been turned into Z's. By the time we made it up to the ninth floor the muscles in our legs were on fire.

"You think they could have picked a lower floor?" he said, casting a glance down the hallway before we darted towards the double doors that were already open.

I ran in scanning the room.

"Dax? Jess?" I yelled but there was no reply. We moved down the hall kicking in the doors and checking every room. They were nowhere to be found.

"Perhaps they got out already."

I nodded. "Yeah."

As we ran down the stairs, I had to ask him. "Why did you come to help?"

"Your friends can be pretty convincing."

"And annoying but that's another story. I'm just glad you guys showed up."

"We had a little help," he replied.

I shot him a look.

"From the dead. Your friend Specs suggested luring them into a truck. We just let them out when we got past the walls. Kind of like having an extra hundred men."

"Smart idea."

“Yeah, I thought so.”

Back on the ground we shot our way out of the building and faced off against the remaining Reapers that had taken up behind two overturned trucks.

“Let’s get the hell out of here.”

“Fuck that. I want their blood,” Elijah spat back.

“It’s not worth it, the Z’s will finish them off.”

The Grim Reapers had dwindled in size from two hundred down to just over a hundred. Bullets were flying back and forth between both sides. I was still trying to figure out where the others had gone when I spotted them. They were rounding the far side of the building.

I nudged Elijah. “Listen, I’ve got to get something from over there, you think you can cover me?”

“You got it.”

“You got a knife?” I asked.

He pulled one from the sheath around his leg.

Elijah shouted to ten of his men to provide cover by using one of the armored trucks to get me over to the middle of Temple Square, and another to provide additional cover. I was literally going to have to expose myself to retrieve the cure from the president's mutilated body. I wasn't sure what scared me more, getting shot in the head by a stray bullet or having to cut into the flesh of our nation's commander-in-chief. No amount of hiding behind the truck was going to keep me from the Reapers that had fanned out. Elijah tossed me an assault rifle. I hopped into the truck and one of his men swung it around and floored it. Bullets were pinging off the steel, and creating cracks in the ballistic glass windows.

I shot a glance at my watch. We had less than an hour to get over to the airport.

As I came up behind the pole that the president had been impaled on, I grimaced. Dry blood streaked the white paint. I tried not to pay attention to the carnage around me, and bullets zipping past my head. I stayed low and had to hope that the two armored trucks would at least block the continual rounds. I glanced up at his face. His head was upright. The pole had been jammed up inside of him and out his throat. Completely unnecessary, barbaric even, but that was Domino. He knew it would send a clear message to everyone.

I looked around his hip for a mark. It was hard to tell what could have been an injection, and what was just bruising from the battering that he'd received. Then I saw it. It was like a bee sting on his left hip. I took the tip of the knife and jammed it inside the flesh. The smell made me gag. As I looked away but continued to slice down I saw Kat in the distance with the others. She was looking directly at me. I'd never felt so uncomfortable, and yet I knew it was what had to be done.

The skin peeled back in one large chunk until I caught sight of the titanium container. It was tiny, no bigger than my thumbnail. To think that held the cure was astonishing. I was just in the process of pulling it out when I felt a bullet nick my skin. It had sliced through the top of my shoulder. I reeled back and began unloading round after round from my assault rifle in the direction of where the shots were coming from. Elijah must have seen I was in trouble as he gestured for them to pull the truck up in front of me. I reached up and pulled out the titanium capsule, skin tissue and all, and pocketed the lot.

After which, I hightailed it back towards Elijah. A lot of his men had already died fighting. There couldn't have been more than half of the fifty still alive. He gave a signal to them men, but most ignored him. That was something about gangs. Their ego was huge. This was going to continue until they either won, or died.

But for us, it was over. It had to be. We only had thirty-five minutes before the choppers would arrive.

"We've got to go."

Elijah grabbed me by my wrist.

"Is that it?"

I nodded. "Yeah. It's the cure."

"Then I'm coming with you."

BLACK HAWK DOWN

Salt Lake City International Airport was located west of Temple Square. It was a fifteen-minute drive on a good day but this wasn't good. It was fucking awful. The sound of gunfire could still be heard echoing in my head as half of us dived in an armored truck driven by Elijah. In the back were four of his men, the rest remained. Maybe they had a death wish?

Up front I rode shotgun. Every few minutes I would cast a glance in the mirror to make sure Dax and the others were still following. On the way I brought Elijah up to speed on how we'd come to learn about the cure. He asked me if I thought it really held a sample that could rid us of the epidemic that was sweeping its way around the world. I told him I was full of as many questions as him. But if it was real, it was now our responsibility to get into the hands of those who might be able to end the horror.

For a few minutes it seemed as if we would make it, that the war we had just left behind would become a faint memory, but that was only wishful thinking. I had turned my head to look in the side mirror when the glass was hit with a bullet. It smashed into pieces and what remained dangled by a thread of cable. Elijah floored it. The engine roared.

"Those Reapers don't give up," he yelled before banging on the metal behind us to alert his men. The station wagon with the others came racing past us. The back window was now gone, and the rear door was riddled with holes. The sound of gunfire could be heard from behind us. Elijah's men had flung open the door and unleashed a furious amount of ammo at the Jeep full of Reapers.

"How far are we now?" I asked.

"At least another ten minutes."

"Shit."

For a moment I thought I couldn't even assist them

as armored trucks weren't built for luxury, they were made to keep the occupants safe. So the windows couldn't be opened. I didn't even have a seat, I was crouched down on the metal floor leaning back when the gunfire started.

So I did the next best thing. I yanked on the handle closest to me and opened wide the side door.

"What the hell are you doing?" Elijah asked.

I gripped a silver handle on the inside and leaned out to return fire. At one point the vehicle swerved and I nearly found myself spitting asphalt. After numerous shots hit the driver of the jeep, the vehicle behind us swerved sharply and flipped sending all five of the occupants to a brutal grave. Smoke and fire erupted making it hard to see what was coming up from behind it. For a brief moment there was relief but it was short-lived when charging through the smoke directly behind them came an armored truck.

"Is that ours?" I heard one of Elijah's men shout.

A return of gunfire answered that.

Now had it only been gunfire, I would have felt

relatively safe. I mean for God's sake we were in a vehicle designed to withstand bullets but that wasn't to be the case. When I spotted one them readying the RPG I knew we were in a whole shit load of trouble. I slammed the door closed. The men in the back must have seen it too as they were unloading round after round in a desperate attempt to kill the Reaper before he fired.

It was futile. We didn't hear the sound of it approaching, only its impact.

The next thing I knew my world had been flipped on its side. The screech of metal, golden sparks flying, and smoke became all I could hear and see. I must have been knocked unconscious because when I awoke the truck had come to a standstill. The sound of fire flickering, amid the heat and black smoke, was disorienting. I immediately felt pain. There was a deep gash on my leg from where metal had torn into it.

"Johnny, give me your hand."

I looked up. It was Elijah reaching down to me. I stretched out my hand and clasped his with what remaining strength I had. Pulled up and out of the steel frame I had a better view of what had happened. The station wagon was pulled to one side, all of them were out with their weapons still in the ready position.

Not far from the truck we were in, I noticed the armored truck that had been in pursuit. It was down in a ditch, the back was open, and bodies lay sprawled on the grass. Whatever had gone down had occurred while I was out cold.

Izzy came rushing over and gave Elijah a hand in carrying me to the car. Halfway there, a fear came over me. *The cure!*

"Hold on. Hold on." I reached into my pocket. I let out a sigh of relief. It was still there. The fear of losing the cure, the one thing we had risked our lives for, overwhelmed me. I could see now why it had been injected into the skin. There was less chance of losing it, and even less of it being stolen. Had one of the scientists self-injected it before the president did? Hopefully I wouldn't need to do that. I glanced at my watch. We had ten minutes until the choppers arrived.

All nine of us piled into the station wagon. It was a tight squeeze and yet I don't think anyone was thinking of comfort at that moment. Elijah hesitated at the door. He looked back towards the road where bodies lay motionless. The blast of the RPG had instantly killed his men.

"Elijah, we need to go," I said.

"Hold on a second." He ran towards the armored vehicle that had followed us. For a moment we lost sight of him in the darkness. A few seconds later he returned carrying the RPG they had used, along with a live round.

"What the hell are you doing?"

"We might need it."

"Yeah, if we were in fucking Afghanistan," Specs hollered.

He stopped at the door, taking one final look at the carnage, smoke, and fire. All around we could see Z's making their way towards us. The place would be swarming in a matter of minutes.

"Elijah," Dax shouted.

He slid in and Baja gunned it out of there. We zigzagged our way around abandoned vehicles and the dead. We hit our fair share of Z's on the final stretch.

"There they are."

I looked out the window, above in the smoke-filled sky I saw the anti-collision lights on the helicopters. They were hovering in the distance.

"Can't this thing go any faster?" Jess yelled

"I'm giving it everything it's got."

"What a piece of shit," Ralphie added.

"Hey! Respect the wagon, bitch," Baja replied.

I wasn't paying attention. All I could think about was getting out of the city. We burned rubber on our approach into the vast parking lot. As we came over a rise in the road, our sense of hope was soon diminished by what we saw next. Among hundreds of cars were countless Z's. It was the most terrifying thing I had ever seen.

"Holy shit," Elijah said, his jaw dropping.

"Why the fuck are they here?" Izzy asked.

"When the shit hits the fan you'd want to get out fast. Return to your family. Who knows?" Specs added.

The car idled at the top of a steep decline as we took in the sight. The vehicle wouldn't stand a chance, we would be crushed if we even attempted to make our way to the airport building.

"Where are they going to land?"

There was barely any space for a vehicle let alone two choppers. They looked to be your typical military Black Hawk helicopters. In the distance we watched as they came down directly above the building.

"They're gonna try and land on the roof," Dax said.

"Can't they see us?" Jess asked.

"Flash the lights," I said.

Baja tapped the high beams several times, hoping they might spot us. Now maybe they saw us, maybe they didn't. Who knew what they could see from their vantage point. That's when we realized what might have made them second-guess coming over to where we were.

"We need to move, there are too many Z's coming," Elijah said, looking through the smashed-out rear window frame. I looked back. They were pouring into the airport from every angle.

"What do we do?" Baja asked.

Dax was quiet. I'd never seen him at a loss for words.

"Dax."

He stared absently.

"Dax!" Baja screamed. "What do we do?"

"How the fuck should I know. Why are you asking me?"

The others looked at each other.

"Go around the other side," Elijah said. "One side has parking, behind the building are planes. There'll be more room."

The noise of the helicopters, the rumble of our vehicle, and the lights were attracting even more Z's on the outskirts of the airport.

"Elijah, we're not going to make it through. That

road is closing up," I said.

"Just do it. Now. We don't have any other option."

Baja looked back at us. A look of helplessness.

"Now!" Elijah yelled.

The station wagon surged forward, Baja hit the pedal to the metal. Each of us readied our weapons and prepared for the worst. The road wound down into the parking lot. The route we were going to take was around the outside. It was less crowded but it still had more than enough Z's to stop us. In the distance I saw the helicopters land, several military personnel jumped out and were firing at Z's that had made their way onto the roof.

"Hit your horn," I yelled.

"No, you'll attract them," Dax said.

"We need to be sure they know we're here."

"I'm pretty damn sure they do. We're the only vehicle in the lot with lights on."

Baja didn't wait for Dax's approval. He hit the horn and the Dixie Lee sound blasted out in all its glory. We jerked forward each time as the vehicle started plowing into one Z after the next. One bounced off the windscreen, smashing it.

"I can't see shit," Baja yelled.

Dax and Specs who were in the front began kicking the crumpled glass out, until it disappeared. Now the vehicle was unprotected in front and back.

"Head in that direction," Elijah yelled. Gunfire erupted in the car, causing our ears to ring as Dax and Specs tried to clear the way ahead of us. It was pointless, there were just too damn many and the car was moving too fast. One flew up onto the hood of the car. With no window to protect us, it reached in. Its jaw snapped. Specs drove his knife into the head. The fear inside was palpable. This was the most insane decision we had made since this whole fuckfest started.

Rounding the building, we could see multiple Boeing 747s docked up against jet bridges. Luggage vehicles were stationed throughout, clothing scattered all over the place. In one area bodies were piled up high

"What now?"

"Head towards that stairwell."

Several of the planes weren't using the enclosed jet bridges that most people used to board planes. They had mobile stairwells that led up to the exit. There was no way we were going to be able to get into the building and make our way to the roof, there were just too many Z's. If we stayed inside the vehicle we would eventually be overrun.

Baja slammed the brakes on in front of the stairwell that led up to a jet with its exit door open. We immediately jumped out and followed Elijah. I'm not sure why we were placing our trust in him other than the fact that he knew the area and out of all us he seemed to know what the hell he was doing. That's the thing about stressful times. There will always be one who manages to stay level-headed. In this moment it was Elijah. We ascended the steps two at time until we reached the opening.

"Get inside."

"What are you doing, Elijah?" Dax asked.

"You'll see."

I rushed inside with the others and began opening fire on the Z's. I had shot one and was in the process of leveling up for another when I saw Elijah raise the RPG towards a Boeing in the distance. Seconds later an explosion erupted, and the shock waves could be felt.

"If they don't know we are here — they do now."

But that wasn't just his plan, he had used it to lure the Z's in the area away from us. To draw them to the far side of the airport building. Flames licked up the side of the Boeing. A giant hole could now be seen.

Elijah fired at several Z's that were making their way up the stairwell.

Inside the plane the others were moving down the aisles clearing out those that had made a home inside. Ralphie and Specs went up front doing the same.

"Get in, Elijah."

He stumbled back into the plane and I yanked the door closed, sealing out the fast-moving Z's.

"Now what?" Jess asked in a panicked state.

"The front of the plane."

We moved forward until we arrived inside the cockpit. I glanced at the countless dials, switches, and handles. Seeing the thick windscreen glass, Dax and I began firing at it until it was riddled with holes. Climbing up, I used the butt of the assault rifle to bang out the glass. We each clambered out onto the nose of the jet, and made our way up to the top of the plane. The glow of the burning plane provided more than enough light to see. Still, the fear of sliding over the edge into the mass of Z's waiting below had all of us nervous. Carefully standing to our feet we began waving with both arms, and yelling as loud as we could.

"Hey!"

We fired rounds into the air. Seeing us, the pilots raced back towards the two Black Hawks and took off. Within a matter of seconds, they were getting closer. Wind whipped at our clothing the nearer they got. Now whether it was a malfunction or pilot error, we'll never know but one of them was in trouble. We heard an alarm, and then in an instant it turned on its side and came down hard. A fiery explosion erupted and our hope diminished.

NORAD

It was like someone had kicked us in the gut. We watched as flames, and black smoke filled the air above the crash. Z's immediately ascended upon the mangled frame. Their bodies caught on fire as they reached for the now dead occupants.

As the other Black Hawk got lower, we crouched down so we wouldn't get blown off the plane. It hovered inches away from the top. Several special ops personnel hopped out and waved us forward. Izzy took Kat. They were the first to get on board. Ralphie followed suit with Jess and Dax. By the time I made it to the helicopter I could immediately see that not that all of us were going. It could only carry up to eleven occupants plus two crew members. There were nine of us, six special ops soldiers, a pilot, and copilot.

"Do you have the cure?" one of the soldiers yelled over the noise of the rotors.

I removed it from my pocket and handed it to him.

"Let's go." He placed a hand on my back and motioned to step into what would have been the final space onboard.

I cast a glance over my shoulder at Baja, Specs, and Elijah. I paused at the edge.

"Get in," he yelled.

"Leave. I'm not going."

The soldier gave a look as if I was insane.

"Johnny, get on," Jess yelled.

"We'll come back for your friends," the soldier yelled.

"They're not my friends. They're family and I won't leave them."

And with that, I stepped away from the helicopter.

I waved them out. "Go, we'll meet you there," I yelled.

Dax's eyes darted between me and the others. He

hesitated for a couple of seconds then he hopped out. "What the hell are you doing, brother? Get on that helicopter."

"I'm not leaving them behind."

"Didn't you hear them? They'll be back."

I scoffed, "They aren't coming back, Dax This was about the president, his daughter, the cure. Not us!"

Dax studied my eyes.

A soldier came over. "What are we doing here? Are you staying or coming?"

The soldier looked notably frustrated.

Dax didn't take his eyes off me as he replied, "Take them. I'm staying."

"Then you might need this." He handed Dax his rifle, and a few mags.

Jess tried to hop off but a soldier pulled her back in.

"Let me go. If they're staying, so am I," Jess spat back.

"Me too," Izzy said trying to push her way off the helicopter.

"Are you all mentally insane?" one of the soldiers said. "We can't let you do that."

"Get off me," Jess cried out.

I went back to the helicopter to help out. "Jess, go with Kat."

"I'm not leaving you."

Ralphie looked torn. "You're not coming?" Ralphie asked.

"We're coming, man — just not now."

The look in Jess's eyes I would never forget.

"Johnny?"

I held both of her hands between mine.

"You're safer with them."

"No. No, you don't get to make that decision."

"Jess. Listen to me."

"No. You listen to me."

And there it was, the strong-willed girl I had fallen for years ago. "I'm staying."

She turned to Izzy, "Stay with Kat, we'll meet up soon."

Izzy shook her head. Jess moved closer to her. "I promise."

The pilot leaned back. "Who the fuck are you people?"

Now I know what I did next was wrong. But you have to understand that what I did was for her best interests. I made the decision for her. I turned to the soldier and told him to take them, including Jess who was still talking to Izzy. The soldier nodded, he gave a signal to the pilot to go, and he jumped back in, slamming the side door behind him.

I crouched down as I moved back. The wind of the rotors whipped at my clothing as my eyes fell on Jess who had now realized what I had done. From behind the window she was yelling to get out but the soldiers kept hold of them. It wasn't just the fact that they would be safer at a military installation, but there wasn't enough room for all of us on the helicopter. I glanced down at the mass of snarling Z's. I couldn't bear the thought of her getting hurt. Now she was surrounded by special ops guys, heading for NORAD. I had no way of knowing what I was sending her into but it had to be better than this.

I rejoined the others and we watched as the Black Hawk flew off into the distance until it became nothing more than a speck. Now there were only five of us. Down below the dead waited; a mass of rotten teeth, and milky white eyes, snarling, moaning, and filling every square inch of the tarmac.

As we crawled back into the aircraft no words were exchanged among us. We knew our next destination but how or if we would reach it was unknown. I had sent them off knowing that I might never see them again. A twinge of regret ate away inside me. Had I made the right decision? If it wasn't, neither Dax nor any of the others brought it up. I wondered what their minds were preoccupied with? I would soon know.

* * *

When dawn broke, and a deep orange sun burned through the tiny aircraft windows, my eyelids flickered, then snapped open. I gasped.

Jess, was my first thought.

The memory of our evening flooded back in. I groaned feeling every bone in my body ache. We had fallen asleep in first class. Elijah was the only other one awake.

"Bad dream?" he asked.

I turned to see him looking out the window.

"Yeah," I said swallowing hard. My mouth was dry.

"Here," he tossed a half drunk bottle of water to me. I twisted off the cap and gulped down every drop.

"Is there more?"

He nodded without looking, then thumbed behind him. I cracked my head from side to side and rolled out of the reclined seat. I stretched my limbs and went in search of the toilet. I snatched up a bottle from a tray that Elijah must have pulled out. Inside, I closed the door behind me, twisted off the cap, leaned over the tiny sink, and ran the water over my head. I swiped my hand across a bloodstained mirror and looked at my ragged face. I was sporting weeks of growth. My eyes were tired with bags beneath them. I gripped the sides of the sink and dropped my head. *You did the right thing. You did the right thing.* I told myself over and over again hoping I might feel better. But now I was beginning to second-guess myself. What had I done? I wasn't thinking straight or was I? I took a piss, and came back out. Elijah was eating a roll.

"Any good?"

"Solid as a rock, but you can't be picky. You want one?"

I nodded. He tossed one to me. It was quiet on the plane and yet we could still hear the moans of the dead from beyond the cockpit's window.

"Why didn't you go?" I asked Elijah. "There was enough room for you."

He swallowed the final piece of his roll and washed it back with water.

"I fuckin' hate the government. I mean. Look at the mess we are in because of them."

"Right, but you could have gone."

"I prefer my chances here." He paused, picking at his teeth. "With you guys."

"You're not going back?" I asked.

"What's there to go back to? Everyone I know is dead now."

I felt a twinge of guilt at the thought that he and the others had risked their lives to help us back at the temple.

"About that." I thanked him.

As we were talking Dax came out, he stared at me and for a minute I thought he was about to rip into me but he didn't.

He ran a hand over his face. "You got a smoke?"

Elijah reached into a bag and tossed him a whole packet from the duty-free.

"Well, look at that. I guess not everything is fucked up."

He glanced at me and I couldn't help but feel somehow responsible. Elijah returned to first class while Dax placed one between his lips and lit it. He blew out a plume of smoke.

"Go on. Say it." I leaned back against the wall of the plane, waiting for him to begin.

"Say what?"

"You know, how I fucked this one up again."

He snorted. "Don't be so hard on yourself." He took another drag. "Though I will say this. She's going to rip you a new one when she sees you. You know that, don't you?"

I nodded, smirking.

"And Izzy?"

Dax dug through a cart of packaged food and small bottles of alcohol. He uncapped a travel size bottle of vodka and downed it. "We probably could use the distance."

With that said he walked back to where the others were. I chewed over his reply before joining them.

Baja lifted his leg and ripped out a morning fart as he stretched. "Shit hot!"

"Baja, you dirty bastard. Did you have to lift your

leg in my direction?" Specs asked.

"Wherever you be, let your wind be free. That's what my grandmother used to say."

We all laughed.

"What?" Baja replied, oblivious to how he sounded.

That morning we ate anything that didn't appear to look as though it had gone off. Which was very little. We checked how much ammo we had left, which was practically none. Though we did have the extra assault rifle, and a few extra mags that one of the soldiers handed Dax.

Outside, we could now see the extent of damage done to the plane. The entire side was torn to pieces by the RPG. The fires still burned, the dead still roamed, and we were over six hundred miles from NORAD. We knew it was time to move out. How we were going to do that was the question. While there appeared to be less Z's outside as most of them had collected around the burning plane, and wandered into entrances in the airport, there were still many on the stairwell and ground shuffling around looking for a flesh breakfast.

Now several ideas were being tossed around between us. Dax of course wanted to just unlock the door, and shoot his way out like the ending to *Butch Cassidy and the Sundance Kid.* Baja had the bright idea of throwing some of the airplane meals out the cockpit window. But he dumped that winning idea when he realized that it would be hard to tell which Z's preferred kosher, vegetarian, or regular meals. The risk was too high, I told him before palming my forehead at the stupidity of it all. The fact is there was no easy way out, we had to go out that door or climb back up on top, hop down onto the wings, and possibly break our legs dropping down from there.

Readying ourselves, I cast a glance out the window to check on how many Z's were directly outside while Baja and Specs argued about who was going to be Butch and who was Sundance. Just as I was about to turn back to the others I spotted a vehicle.

"Hey guys. Guys. Take a look at this."

They all took a porthole.

An armored vehicle was plowing its way through Z's. We heard a gun going off several times. The noise it was making was beginning to attract the Z's lingering around the station wagon. Like the Pied Piper of Hamelin it was leading them. Driving a slow enough speed to make them follow.

"What do you make of that?"

"Hell knows."

"You think it's the Reapers?"

"Possibly."

"Well, either way. They've just made it a little bit easier to get out. Look."

On the stairwell the Z's were descending following the herd. We gave it another five minutes before Dax broke the seal on the door and yanked it wide. Light poured in and we breathed the smell of smoke.

"Ah, nothing like a bit of fresh air," Baja said sniffing the air as he stepped out. The Z's that were still on the steps turned their milky white eyes on us.

"I got this," Specs said.

"No. I do," Baja said, pushing him to one side.

"Dude, I told you, I'm Butch, you're Sundance."

"The fuck I am, you're the one with the dirty mustache."

"Look guys, who gives a crap, from what I remember they both came out shooting," I said.

Baja nodded. Specs agreed. All the while a Z was making its way up. Both of them turned at the same time and fired two rounds into its head. "Hell yeah!"

That began our push towards the car at the bottom of the stairwell. We moved forward with purpose, only taking out those that were an immediate threat.

"Baja, you better have the keys," Dax yelled as he peppered the heads of three zombies.

"Of course I do, you penis." He yanked them out of his pocket so hard they flew out of his hands. All we could do was watch as they soared through air. Then Specs performing his best Air Jordan move jumped up and caught them — barely.

I exhaled hard with relief and fired a round into a Z's skull.

"That's why I'm Butch, bitch!" Specs replied looking all pleased with himself.

"Give me those, you moron." Dax snatched the keys out of Specs's hand and charged ahead. "I swear I'm going to kill you both before these flesh-chewing freaks do."

A few more rounds and we were back inside the station wagon. After a bit of an argument over who should be driving, Baja slipped over into the driver's passenger side under the threat that if he fucked up, Dax was going to cut off his balls and hang them from the mirror like a pair of furry dice.

"Yeah, yeah, I've got this."

"That's what you said last time," Dax spat back.

Baja put the key in and twisted. The engine coughed to life then went dead. He tried again. It coughed and spluttered.

"Please tell me you didn't leave the lights on?" I

asked.

"No!" he paused. "I don't think I did. I mean in all the hurry, it's kind of possible."

"Shit, Baja."

"Well, how the hell did I know we were going to have to use it again?"

All of us were shooting out of the windows as more Z's shifted their gaze on us and decided the armored vehicle was just too far to shuffle for breakfast.

"Get it started. Now!"

"What the fuck do you think I'm doing, jerking off?"

Baja began speaking to the car as if it was a sick lover of his. "C'mon baby, don't fail me now. Me and you go way back, or at least I do with your cousin, or perhaps it's your…"

"Baja," Dax yelled growing impatient.

Baja took a deep breath and tried again. This time it roared to life and he revved the engine hard. "Ooooh, that's my girl."

"How much gas we got?" Specs asked.

Baja tapped the gas gauge. "Half a tank."

"That'll do for now."

"Alright, if you're done giving foreplay to your girlfriend, can you get us the hell out of here?" Elijah shouted.

Baja gunned the engine and we tore away from the zombie-infested lot. As we rounded the building a vast majority of the Z's had shifted to one side of the lot, no doubt following the noise and gunfire of the armored truck that was now nowhere to be seen. We sped up an incline that led away from the airport.

Upon reaching the crest of the steep hill we saw in the distance an armored vehicle parked sideways. Behind it a trail of mud spread across the highway as though it had taken a shortcut across a field. Baja brought the car down to a crawl as we approached it.

"Be ready," Dax said as he brought his gun up.

From around the corner of the armored truck came a figure.

"Who the hell is that?" Elijah asked, squinting because of the glare from the morning sun.

I smiled. "Benjamin."

He stood there, Glock in hand, assault rifle over his back. I tapped Baja on the shoulder and he pulled up beside him.

"Room for one more?" he asked.

I was about to reply when Baja spoke up. "Depends, can you handle yourself?"

Without even looking, Ben brought up his Glock to the side and fired a round directly into an approaching Z's head. He didn't even blink.

Baja sniffed hard. "Beginner's luck."

We laughed and opened the door for him. When he got in he turned to his right and looked directly at Elijah.

"Oh, hell no," Benjamin said.

"Shit," Elijah said, swiping his hand over his head.

"Do you guys know each other?" I asked.

They both said the same thing at the same time.

"You could say that."

I had a feeling we were about to learn a lot about these two. Baja breathed in deeply, as we peeled away. As we did he reached down by his side and lifted up the armrest compartment. He shot a glance down and then looked back at the road.

"Where you guys heading?" Benjamin asked.

"NORAD."

He shook his head. "I don't know why I asked."

Baja reached down and pulled out an old tape. "What do we have here?" he said.

"They still do tapes?"

Baja chuckled to himself. "They did in 1992, and I think you're gonna love this one."

I saw the words *Geto Boys* scribbled in marker pen on the tape.

He tossed it into the tape player and switched it on. All of us waited with bated breath for what was about to play. When I heard it, I began to laugh. The first song was *Damn It Feels Good To Be A Gangsta.*

Baja breathed in deeply. "I think I can feel a road trip coming on," he said before leaning back and letting the beat of the music take over.

So there we were on our way to meet up with Jess, Izzy, and Ralphie at the Cheyenne Mountain Complex in Colorado. There was no way of knowing what we'd find when we arrived, or even if we would make it. I guess in a strange twist of fate we were now placing our faith in a government that had let us down; in a cure that we weren't sure was real.

We had gained new allies, and brought together two men who were former enemies. If there was hope for them, perhaps there was hope for humanity.

Until then, we will choose to stand between what remains and all that might come to kill.

We may not be the fastest or strongest.

We might not have what it takes to survive.

But we're full of heart, and that's enough.

We are, the Renegades.

A PLEA

Thank you for reading The Renegades 2: Aftermath. If you enjoyed the book, I would really appreciate it if you would consider leaving a review. I can't stress how helpful this is in helping other readers decide if they should give it a shot. Reviews from readers like you are the best recommendation a book can have. Without reviews, an author's books are virtually invisible on the retail sites. It also lets me know what you liked. You can leave a review by visiting the book's page. I would greatly appreciate it. It only takes a couple of seconds.

Thank you — **Jack Hunt**

NEWSLETTER

Thank you for buying The Renegades, published by Direct Response Publishing.

Go here to receive special offers, bonus content, and news about new Jack Hunt's books. Sign up for the newsletter. http://www.jackhuntbooks.com

JACK HUNT

Jack Hunt is the author of horror, sci-fi and post-apocalyptic novels. Jack lives on the East coast of North America. When he's not writing, he's engaged in dubious activities and general shenanigans. He invites you to contact him, send him lots of money and turn all his books into movies.

If he doesn't reply straight away, he's probably running away from a Zombie, chatting with his drug dealer or having a dump. Either way, he will respond when he's good and ready unless of course you are the FBI in which case you'll never hear from him.

Made in United States
Orlando, FL
22 September 2023

37186406R10224